MEGAHERO

THE TERRIBLE TRICKS OF
MISS TAKE

STEVE BARLOW • STEVE SKIDMORE
ILLUSTRATED BY PIPI SPOSITO

D0248428

Franklin Watts
First published in Great Britain in 2020
by The Watts Publishing Group

Text © Steve Barlow and Steve Skidmore 2020
Illustrations © Franklin Watts 2020
Design: Cathryn Gilbert

ISBN 978 1 4451 7009 1
ebook ISBN 978 1 4451 7011 4
Library ebook ISBN 978 1 4451 7010 7

1 3 5 7 9 10 8 6 4 2

Printed in Great Britain

MIX
Paper from
responsible sources
FSC
www.fsc.org
FSC® C104740

HOW TO BE A MEGAHERO

Some superheroes can read books with their X-ray vision without opening the covers or even when they're in a different room ...

Others can read them while flying through the air or stopping a runaway train.

But that stuff *IS* just small potatoes to you, because you're not a superhero. You're a *MEGAHERO*!

YES, this book is about **YOU**! And you don't just read it to the end and then stop. You read a bit: then you make a choice that takes you to a different part of the book. You might jump from Section 3 to 47 or 28!

If you make a good choice, *GREAT!*

BUUUUUUT ...

If you make the wrong choice ... *DA-DA-DAAAH!* **ALL KINDS OF BAD STUFF WILL HAPPEN.**

Too bad! It's no good turning green and tearing your shirt off. You'll just have to start again. But that won't happen, will it?

Because you're not a zero, or even a superhero. You are ... *MEGAHERO*!

You are a **BRILLIANT INVENTOR** — but one day **THE SUPER PARTICLE-ACCELERATING COSMIC RAY COLLIDER** you'd made out of old drinks cans, lawnmower parts and a mini black hole went critical and scrambled your molecules (nasty!). When you finally stopped screaming, smoking and bouncing off the walls, you found your body had changed! Now you can transform into any person, creature or object. *How awesome is that?!!!*

You communicate with your *MEGACOMPUTER* companion, **PAL**, through your *MEGASHADES* sunglasses (which make you look pretty COOL, too). **PAL** controls the things you turn into and *almost hardly ever crashes and has to be turned off and on again!* This works perfectly — unless you have a bad WIFI signal, or **PAL** gets something wrong — but hey! That's computers for you, right?

Like all heroes, your job is to SAVE THE WORLD from **BADDIES AND THEIR EVIL SCHEMES**. But be back in time for supper. Even *MEGAHEROES* have to eat …

Go to 1.

1

You are at the **GALACTIC COMICS CONVENTION**, signing autographs for your many fans. As you admire the top exhibit at the convention — a priceless, mint-condition copy of the first ever Superduperman comic — six ray-gun-toting "ALIENS" appear.

The audience applauds, thinking that this is all part of the show. But the applause turns to screams as the "ALIENS" spray gas from their "RAY GUNS". Panic-stricken fans stampede for the exits.

To tackle the "ALIENS", go to 18.
To change into a giant electric fan, go to 27.

2

The next day, having been released by an angry
Herr Dresser, you decide to find out what
Miss Take is plotting. You sneak onto the
St. Mammon's coach, climb onto the luggage rack
and become a backpack.

As the pupils file on, you spot the girl who
carried out the robbery at the Louvre. She sits
on the back seat of the coach with four friends.
An ID badge hangs around her neck.

As the coach sets off, the girl and her friends
mutter together. You only hear bits of their
conversation.

"Munich next," says one.

"And the white bear," says another.

Irma Rongun angrily shushes them. She seems
to be their leader.

*Is she the mysterious **Miss Take?*** you wonder.

The coach pulls in at a service area.

To stay on the coach, go to 30.

**To get to Munich ahead of the school party,
go to 15.**

3

You turn into a dragonfly and follow the girl into the pyramid. You stay close as she skims through the museum, dodging sensor beams.

The masked girl stops in front of a painting and disables the alarms.

"THAT'S THE MINOR LISA," whispers PAL. "IT'S THE MONA LISA AS A CHILD. IT'S WORTH A MINT!"

The girl takes out a sharp knife and cuts the canvas from its frame.

To follow the thief out of the museum, go to 23.

To arrest her, go to 34.

Luckily, the photographer covering the exhibition has taken a picture of the band. You upload this to PAL, who runs it through the St. Mammon's registration files. This confirms that "**Miss Take**" is Irma Rongun. But you need to catch her red-handed to give **Herr Dresser** the proof he needs.

"I've spotted a pattern," you tell PAL. "The **Superduperman** comic — the Minor Lisa — a teddy — all stuff kids like. The school trip is going to Venice next. Is there anything there to tempt **Miss Take**?"

"YES," says PAL. "THERE'S AN EXHIBITION OF GAMES CONSOLES, INCLUDING THE WORLD'S MOST EXPENSIVE ONE — THE BILLIONAIRES' CONSOLE. IT HAS A SOLID GOLD CASE SMOTHERED WITH PRECIOUS STONES AND DIAMOND HAND-CONTROLLERS."

You nod. "That's what **Miss Take** must be after."

To fly to Venice with the school party, go to 13.

To get there first, go to 29.

5

You fly through the open back door and into the exhibition hall just as **Miss Take** sets off a smoke grenade and steals the Billionaires' Console. You become human and give chase as she and her accomplices escape from the crowded building on BMX bikes. You struggle to follow.

To stay in human form, go to 16.

To turn into an animal that can barge through the crowd, go to 25.

6

"Make me a bat!" you tell PAL.

You turn into a piece of willow with a handle at one end.

"Not a **CRICKET** bat! A **FLYING** bat!"

"OK, OK, DON'T GET IN A FLAP ..."

Flying above the panicking crowd, you follow the "**ALIENS**" out of the convention hall, across the street and into an elevated metro station.

Before you can arrest them, a train arrives. The "**ALIENS**" get on it.

To turn into a sports car, go to 19.

To follow the train as a bat, go to 22.

The band has stopped playing. You realise that the "**MUSICIANS**" are *Miss Take* and her gang.

Miss Take snatches the Elvis Teddy from its stand.

"Bad guess, *MEGAHERO*!" she sneers. "My team spotted your ridiculous rag-doll disguise ages ago. *Bear* with me while I detonate this cuteness grenade!"

She throws a metal canister that bursts at your feet.

The shocked people suddenly come to life and stare soppily at your cute rag-doll disguise.

"*OOOOH*, so squishy!" they simper.

"Gorgeous!"

"Adorable!"

Moments later, you are cuddled half to death as *Miss Take* and her gang make their escape.

To turn into a tracker dog, go to 17.

To find out who was in the band, go to 4.

8

You sneak into the zoo in human form. But you are immediately spotted by security guards, who assume you are up to no good. They move in to arrest you.

You wonder whether you should try to get away from them, or turn into something they can't move.

To change into a novelty big green frog litter bin, go to 32.

To try to escape, go to 14.

9

Becoming human, you stride up to the front doors. A security guard asks for your ticket.

"I don't have one," you say. "Let me through — I'm *MEGAHERO*!"

"Si, Signore, and I am the Emperor Napoleon."

You try and push past the guard. He calls for backup. You struggle. Police arrest you as **Miss Take** and her accomplices burst out of the hall with their loot and make their escape.

What an arresting development! *Go back to 1.*

10

You switch to human form and find a guard. You try to explain what you have seen, but unfortunately you don't speak French. Before the guard can understand what you are saying, alarm bells are ringing. More guards race towards the doors. The gang has struck — you are too late!

You should have learned to *parlez français*!
Go back to 1.

11

You drop into the pit full of sleeping bears. Unfortunately, one of them is still awake. It lumbers forward and grabs you in a bear hug.

"PAL," you gasp, "I think this bear fancies me ..."

At that moment, **Miss Take** and her gang appear overhead on a flying carpet drone. Turning into a tiny monkey to escape the disappointed bear, you wriggle out of the bear hug and climb quickly out of the pit and follow.

The gang leaves the carpet to stalk the unicorn. How can you save it?

To turn into a lion, go to 26.

To turn into an orangutan, go to 40.

To turn into another unicorn, go to 21.

The next day, you meet **Herr Dresser** of Interpol, the international police agency that tracks criminals worldwide.

"The suspects attend St. Mammon's Private Academy for Privileged Children," he says. "They are on a school trip. Everywhere they visit, valuables go missing."

"Can't you just hold them until someone owns up?" you say. "Tell them it's their own time they're wasting …"

"No," says **Herr Dresser**. "The one you caught is saying nothing. Anyway, these are all children of very important people. We can't lock them up without proof. We believe the ringleader calls herself '*Miss Take*'."

"I'll prove they're guilty," you say. "Where are they going next?"

"To Paris."

When the St. Mammon's party arrives in Paris, you are waiting to spy on them.

To sneak onto their coach, go to 28.

To disguise yourself as a piece of luggage, go to 20.

To pretend to be a stray dog, go to 38.

13

"The flight is full," you tell PAL. "I'll travel in the hold. Do you know the airport code for Venice?"

"SURE," says PAL. "IT'S VNC."

PAL turns you into an air freight parcel. You are loaded onto a plane. The flight takes longer than expected, but eventually you are unloaded in Venice, Florida.

Wrong Venice! *Go back to 1.*

14

You turn into a seal and wriggle away. The guards can't get hold of your slippery coat.

You smell water nearby and flop towards it.

SPLASH!

I'm safe now, you think.

Unfortunately, you're wrong. You've fallen into the polar bear enclosure — and they eat seals!

DA-DA-DAAAH!

You've sealed your fate! **Go back to 1.**

15

Leaving the coach, you make your way to an empty field and turn into a **EUROCOPTER H155** helicopter. You take off and head east.

"WHERE ARE YOU GOING?" asks PAL.

"Munich," you reply. "I heard **Miss Take** talking to her gang on the coach — I think they're going to steal a polar bear!"

To report to Interpol, go to 39.

To head for Munich Zoo, go to 43.

To head for the Munich tourist information office, go to 24.

16

Police are running towards the exhibition hall. You accidentally barge into one. "I'm *MEGAHERO*!" you shout. "Out of my way!"

The startled policeman mistakes you for one of the thieves and tasers you. By the time you come round, **Miss Take** and her gang are long gone.

Go to 45.

17

You get the scent of **Miss Take** and her gang from the band's discarded instruments, and quickly follow it.

You spot **Miss Take** crossing the main square, the Marienplatz and give chase — but the sly schoolgirl hurls a stink bomb that bursts in front of you. Your doggy scent glands overload, and you quickly switch back to human form. By the time your eyes have stopped watering, **Miss Take** and her crew have disappeared.

That girl's not to be sniffed at!
Go back to 1.

18

You charge towards the "ALIENS". They fire their ray guns at you. The gas makes you suddenly desperate for a wee.

Outside the toilet, you hop about as you queue with other victims. By the time you get back, the "ALIENS" have stolen the priceless Superduperman comic and escaped.

You've been caught short! Go back to 1.

19

"PAL," you yell, "make me a **FERRARI**!"

Tyres squealing and engine revving, you try to follow the train. But the road turns away from the metro tracks. Traffic slows you down. You eventually grind to a halt as the thieves get away.

You're in a jam! Go back to 1.

20

You become a suitcase and wait on the pavement to be loaded onto a coach.

Sometime later, you are taken out again and are amazed to find yourself at the airport! You've been loaded onto the wrong coach! Before you can contact PAL, you are put through an X-ray machine. This damages your shades' delicate circuits. You are helpless as you are packed into the hold of a plane heading for Bangkok.

You silly baggage! *Go back to 1.*

21

You gallop into the paddock, scattering the gang, and stand beside the real unicorn.

"I don't know which to steal," moans **Miss Take**. "There's only room on the carpet for one." She points at you. "Take that one!"

The carpet flies out of the zoo and lands beside a truck. The gang open the door to shoo you in — and you spot all the loot they have already stolen inside.

You return to human form. "You've made a big mistake, **Miss Take**," you chuckle. You become a steel cage surrounding the gang and their truck.

"Call **Herr Dresser**," you tell PAL. "I have all the proof he needs."

Go to 50.

22

Using your bat's speed, you pass the train and wait at the next station.

Six passengers get off the train. For a moment, you think these are innocent schoolchildren — until you spot an alien costume that one has stuffed into his backpack. It's time to make an arrest!

To become human, go to 37.

To turn into a pair of handcuffs, go to 46.

23

You follow the thief as she rejoins her friends. They all jump into the waiting taxi. You try to follow, but in the darkness you fly into a spider's web. You struggle helplessly as the spider wraps you in its silk.

DA-DA-DAAAH!

You're all tied up! Go back to 1.

24

You land in Munich and head for the nearest tourist information office.

"WHY ARE WE HERE?" asks PAL.

"I've been thinking. I could be wrong about the polar bear. **Miss Take** may be after another kind of bear."

You spot a poster advertising an exhibition at the Teddy Bear Museum.

"Listen," you tell PAL. "The top exhibit is a bear dressed as Elvis, in a white suit with real diamonds. It's worth a fortune."

That afternoon, having become a human-sized rag-doll, you watch as an excited crowd files into the museum. A photographer is wandering around snapping photos of guests, and a German oompah brass band is playing non-stop.

The Elvis teddy is on display, surrounded by admirers.

Nearby stands a giant teddy. *I'll bet that's where **Miss Take** is hiding*, you think.

To confront **Miss Take**, go to 49.

To wait for her to make her move, go to 35.

You become a ram. Barging pedestrians aside with your massive curved horns, you chase the thieves through the narrow streets of Venice.

The fleeing wrongdoers abandon their bikes at a canal wharf and scramble on board a rocket-propelled gondola. It zooms away. You're going too fast to stop, and tumble into the canal. Rams are poor swimmers, so ...

"Quick, PAL!" you cry. "Turn me into a tern!"

PAL is confused. "I CAN'T TURN YOU INTO A TURN!"

"Not a **TURN**, a **TERN**. A kind of seabird."

"A KIND OF SEABIRD YOU TURN INTO A TURN? WHAT DOES THAT EVEN MEAN?"

"*BUBBLE, BUBBLE, BUBBLE ...*"

DA-DA-DAAAH!

You've got that sinking feeling. *Go back to 1.*

You roar and spring to the attack.

Instantly, **Miss Take** and her accomplices fall to their knees and wring their hands. "Spare us," they wail. "We're only poor, innocent children!"

You hesitate, and in that moment, **Miss Take** explodes a sleeping-gas grenade under your nose.

By the time you wake up, you are in the zookeepers' nets — and the unicorn is gone!

Sleeping on the job again? *Go back to 1.*

"PAL," you cry, "turn me into a fan."

You turn into a gloomy teenager wearing a torn "I ♥ COMMIX" T-shirt.

"An **ELECTRIC FAN**!" you yell. "A big one!"

"OK," says PAL, "DON'T GET THE WIND UP."

Your spinning blades blow the gas away. But while you have been distracted, the **"ALIENS"** have stolen the Superduperman comic and are escaping down the stairs leading to the street. You must give chase at once!

To turn into a cheetah, go to 33.
To turn into a bat, go to 6.
To turn into a gibbon, go to 41.

You sneak on board the St. Mammon's coach when nobody is looking and change into a nodding tiger ornament. You sit on the dashboard at the front to spy on the schoolchildren.

You have a boring day, nodding away while the pupils visit famous landmarks. Nobody does any thieving. Eventually, the coach parks outside the school party's hotel and the students head inside.

To take this opportunity for some refreshment, go to 42.

To keep watch on the hotel, go to 47.

"Turn me into a white stork," you tell PAL.

Immediately, you become a large bird with a two-metre wingspan. You flap into the air and head south.

Your powerful wings carry you over the mountains. The following day you land in Venice, outside the hall where the exhibition of games consoles is being held. The square is crowded and a balloon-seller is standing nearby.

To become one of his balloons, go to 44.
To become a pigeon, go to 36.

As the pupils stream off the coach, one of them grabs you.

"Look! I've got Dotty Digby's backpack!" he chortles. He throws you onto the back of a passing garbage truck. "Hey, Dotty! Your backpack's hitched a ride." His friends snicker and catcall.

Lying on top of the rubbish, you see a blonde girl patting a backpack that looks exactly like you.

"You're always trying to bully me, Coggins, you beast! But you're wrong!" she says smugly. "I don't know whose backpack you just chucked on that cart, but it's not mine. Mine's right here!" Coggins and his friends look disappointed.

That's all you hear. At this moment, the garbage compactor starts working ...

DA-DA-DAAAH!
You're feeling the SQUEEEEZE ...
Go back to 1.

You admire the unicorn strutting around its paddock, but you keep your eyes open for trouble, too. Security at the zoo seems tight, and there is no sign of **Miss Take**.

When the zoo is about to close, you hide in the toilets until all the visitors have gone. Then you make a beeline for the unicorn's enclosure. You must get there quickly, before **Miss Take** can strike.

Unfortunately, the quickest routes to the unicorn paddock are through the tigers' cage or across a large bear pit.

To take a chance with the tigers, go to 48.

To drop into the bear pit, go to 11.

32

The guards can't move you. You sit there smugly while they argue, until they get a radio call. The unicorn has been stolen while you've been doing nothing. You're too late!

Don't just stand there! *Go back to 1.*

33

Your appearance as a big cat causes panic.

Screaming fans get in your way and block your path to the escaping "**ALIENS**"!

You made a bad choice!

To turn into a bat, go to 6.
To turn into a gibbon, go to 41.

34

You change to human form and point at the startled thief. "Stop right there!"

But your sudden appearance sets off the alarms. Roller shutters lower to cover every exit from the gallery. The thief flies through a narrowing gap on a hoverboard but you are too slow to follow. You are trapped, and soon you find yourself being manhandled by angry guards.

Go to 2.

A child throws its arms around you. "Oooh, Mummy, can we buy this rag-doll?"

"It's too big, darling," says the kid's mother. "Let go." But the kid doesn't.

You forget you are in disguise. "Let go, kid," you growl. "Listen to your mother."

The child starts screaming. So does its mother. She beats you up with her handbag.

As you cower from her blows, there is a flash of light that stuns and shocks the crowd into silence.

Go to 7.

As a pigeon, you can patrol the skies above the exhibition hall and move quickly if something happens; plus you get free grain from friendly tourists.

You see the St. Mammon's pupils arrive at the Games Console Exhibition.

To sneak into the exhibition through the back door, go to 5.

To go in through the front entrance, go to 9.

You turn back into human form.

"You're under arrest," you tell the children.

"Oh, have mercy!" squeals one kid.

"I'm so scared," wails another.

An old lady shuffles menacingly towards you.
"Stop pestering those poor kids!" She goes for
you with her umbrella while your suspects leg it.

Brolly poor show! *Go back to 1.*

38

You hang around watching the coach. When it sets off you follow, only to lose it briefly in traffic. Spotting it again, you give chase.

Eventually, the coach stops — and a load of old age pensioners get off. Wrong coach!

You are so upset, you don't notice the dog catcher sneaking up behind you.

Dog gone it! *Go back to 1.*

39

You arrive in Munich and ask PAL to call **Herr Dresser**.

"A POLAR BEAR?" he demands. "ARE YOU CRAZY?" But eventually, he agrees to stake out the zoo.

You join the German police as they keep watch ... but nothing happens.

At midnight, your phone rings. "You buffoon!" rages **Herr Dresser**. "**Miss Take** has robbed the Teddy Bear Museum — while you were wasting time watching the zoo! You're fired!"

You can't bear it! *Go back to 1.*

40

You shuffle towards the gang, going "***OOOK!***" in a menacing way.

Miss Take reaches into her bag and pulls out a banana. "Look what I've got for a good boy!" she coos. "There's plenty more where that came from!" She throws it to you.

Automatically, you reach out to catch it, and an electric shock knocks you out. By the time you wake up, **Miss Take** and her gang have escaped.

You've fallen for the old electric banana trick! *Go back to 1.*

41

You change into a gibbon and chase the **"ALIENS"** by swinging from light fittings, **"THIS WAY"** signs and other dangling stuff. But the **"ALIENS"** take a corridor with a low ceiling. With nothing to swing from, you aren't fast enough to keep up. You're going to have to change!

Go to 6.

42

You are in a small café enjoying a cola when you get a phone call from a furious **Herr Dresser**.

"I'm at the Louvre museum!" he rages. "While you've been sitting around, the thieves have struck! You're off the case!"

Go back to 1.

43

Arriving at the zoo, you land and sneak into the grounds.

"YOU NEED AN ANIMAL DISGUISE," says PAL.

Soon you are a sloth, hanging upside down from a branch. A zookeeper spots you and runs off.

Sloths are very good at keeping still and watching. You wait.

The keeper, having mistaken you for an escaped zoo animal, comes back with a tranquilliser gun. He fires a dart into your hairy sloth butt.

You wake up to find that **Miss Take** has struck again!

Hanging around won't get you anywhere!
Go back to 1.

You become a *MEGAHERO* balloon (what else?) and attach yourself to the balloon seller's bundle. Floating above the crowds, you watch the St. Mammon's pupils go into the exhibition.

Shortly afterwards, five masked children burst out of the front door, leap onto BMX bikes, and speed away, pursued by security guards. They race towards the balloon seller, who lets go of his balloons and flees. You float helplessly away — into the path of a short-sighted seagull. Its sharp beak punctures you. You have an uncontrollable leak!

How embarrassing! *Go back to 1.*

By the time the Italian police let you go, you are in despair.

"NEWS JUST IN," says PAL. "A REAL LIVE UNICORN HAS BEEN DISCOVERED IN A REMOTE VALLEY IN PAKISTAN. IT'S BEEN TAKEN TO LAHORE ZOO — AND THAT'S WHERE THE ST. MAMMON'S PARTY IS GOING NEXT."

This is your last chance to catch **Miss Take**. You turn into a **EUROFIGHTER TYPHOON** military jet and head for Pakistan. Some hours later, you arrive in Lahore.

To sneak into the zoo after dark, go to 8.

To visit the zoo during the day as a tourist, go to 31.

You drop out of the sky and snap around the wrists of one of the schoolchildren. Her struggles to escape are in vain, but while you are holding her prisoner, the others escape.

Go to 12.

You turn into a mobile coffee stall and watch the hotel.

An hour later, five foxy figures leave via the staff entrance. A taxi picks them up. You start your engine and follow.

The taxi pulls up outside the Louvre museum. The gang, wearing masks, gets out. The taxi waits as the thieves remove a triangular pane of glass from the pyramid standing in front of the entrance. One of the girls takes a jet-propelled hoverboard out of her backpack and drops through the gap.

To follow, go to 3.
To go for help, go to 10.

48

You enter the tiger cage and tiptoe towards the back door.

Unfortunately, one of the tigers is a very light sleeper. It leaps up, snarling, and pounces.

DA-DA-DAAAH!

OOER — you'll have to change your name to Claude. *Go back to 1.*

Forgetting that you are in disguise, you throw yourself on the giant teddy.

Kids scream at the sight of a rag-doll coming to life. They scream even louder as the rag-doll pulls the teddy's head off. You dig out handfuls of stuffing before you realise that **Miss Take** isn't inside the giant Teddy.

Security guards arrive and grab you. You are still being interrogated when news comes through on their radios — **Miss Take** has stolen the Elvis teddy and got clean away.

That's knocked the stuffing out of you!
Go back to 1.

Interpol officers arrive and take the gang into custody.

Herr Dresser claps you on the back. "She'll get 300 years' detention for this!" he gloats.

You look through the one-way glass into the cell, where a warder is talking to **Miss Take**.

"You're going to stand there and think about what you did ..."

"She'll have plenty of time to regret her **Miss** Deeds," you say. "She thought she could fool me. She **Miss** Calculated. Her whole plan has **Miss** Fired."

"**BA-DUM – TISH!**" says PAL.

The End!

I HERO

MEGAHERO

THE DREADFUL DEEDS OF
DINASAW

Steve Barlow · Steve Skidmore
Illustrated by Pipi Sposito

EDGE

Following another successful mission, you are in a café in Washington DC checking the news on your *MEGA CELLPHONE* when a BREAKING NEWS story appears ...

A GIANT FLYING REPTILE APPARENTLY MADE OF SCRAPYARD JUNK, WHICH OBSERVERS HAVE INSTANTLY DUBBED THE TERROR-SOAR, HAS APPEARED IN THE SKIES ABOVE THE NATION'S CAPITAL.

To ignore the story, go to 14.
To investigate it, go to 33.

CONTINUE THE ADVENTURE IN:

THE DREADFUL DEEDS OF
DINASAW

About the 2Steves

"The 2Steves" are
Britain's most popular
writing double act for
young people, specialising
in comedy and adventure.
They perform regularly in
schools and libraries, and at festivals, taking the
power of words and story to audiences of all ages.

Together they have written many books, including the
I HERO Immortals and *iHorror* series.

About the illustrator:
Pipi Sposito

Pipi was born in Buenos Aires in
the fabulous 60's and has always
drawn. As a little child, he used
to make modelling clay figures, too.
At the age of 19 he found out
he could earn a living by drawing. He now develops
cartoons and children's illustrations in different
artistic styles, and also 3D figures, puppets and
caricatures. Pipi always listens to music when he works.

Have you completed these I HERO adventures?

I HERO Immortals — more to enjoy!

Dinosaur Hunter
978 1 4451 6963 7 pb
978 1 4451 6964 4 ebook

Fairy
978 1 4451 6969 9 pb
978 1 4451 6971 2 ebook

Knight
978 1 4451 6957 6 pb
978 1 4451 6959 0 ebook

Pirate Queen
978 1 4451 6954 5 pb
978 1 4451 6955 2 ebook

Samurai
978 1 4451 6960 6 pb
978 1 4451 6962 0 ebook

Witch
978 1 4451 6966 8 pb
978 1 4451 6967 5 ebook

Defeat all the baddies in Toons:

Killer Custard
978 1 4451 5930 0 pb
978 1 4451 5931 7 ebook

Robin Hamster
978 1 4451 5921 8 pb
978 1 4451 5922 5 ebook

Enter the Penguin
978 1 4451 5924 9 pb
978 1 4451 5925 6 ebook

Kung Fu Kitten
978 1 4451 5918 8 pb
978 1 4451 5919 5 ebook

Also by the 2Steves...

GALAXY
FOOTBALL CUP

978 1 4451 5985 0 hb
978 1 4451 5986 7 pb

MOVIE STAR
SET-UP

978 1 4451 5976 8 hb
978 14451 5977 5 pb

ROBOT
RAMPAGE

978 1 4451 5982 9 hb
978 1 4451 5983 6 pb

SMALL
WORLD

978 1 4451 5972 0 hb
978 1 4451 5971 3 pb

SPACE
CHASE

978 1 4451 5892 1 hb
978 1 4451 5891 4 pb

SPACE
PIRATES

978 1 4451 5988 1 hb
9781 4451 5989 8 pb

SPACE
RAP

978 1 4451 5973 7 hb
978 1 4451 5974 4 pb

WEB
WORLD

978 1 4451 5979 9 hb
978 1 4451 5980 5 pb

Dedication

Dedicated once again to our many friends around the world, who constantly call, write and overflow our email inboxes with mirth and merriment and bend our ears in noisy pubs to tell us their latest stories!

Among these, special mentions must go to
Derek Searle, John Wilson,
Nick Potts, Malcolm Corby, Michael Briggs
Carol Coleman, Pam Leaper, Cheryl Mulryne, Stewart Milner,
Heather Walton, Alan Bland, Peter Halls,
Paul Weinberg and Robin Ladd
for their imagination, sense of humour and consistent supply!

Also our warmest thanks go to the rest of the team that helped make this publication possible
Derek & John

...and for starters....

When you're sitting in a tiresome meeting, remember the phrase "DEJA MOO"

Its the feeling that you've heard this bullshit somewhere before!

<u>Bury Me With My Money!</u>

There was a Scottish Jewish chartered accountant who had worked all of his life and had saved all of his money. He was a real miser when it came to his money. He loved money more than just about anything, and just before he died, he said to his wife, "Now listen, when I die, I want you to take all my money and place it in the casket with me. I wanna take my money to the after life. I've put it in my will"

So he got his wife to promise him with all her heart that when he died, she would put all the money in the casket with him.

Well, one day he died. He was stretched out in the casket, the wife was sitting there in black next to her closest friend. When they finished the ceremony, just before the undertakers got ready to close the casket, the wife said "Wait just a minute!"

She had a shoe box with her, she came over with the box and placed it in the casket. Then the undertakers locked the casket down and rolled it away.

Her friend said, "I hope you weren't crazy enough to put all that money in the casket."

She said, "Yes, I promised. I'm an obedient Jewish wife.
I promised him that I was going to put that money in that casket with him."

"You mean to tell me you put every cent of his money in the casket with him?"

"I sure did," said the wife. "I got it all together, put it into my account and I wrote him a cheque."

Question: What is a bastard exactly?

Quite often we ask ourselves "hard to answer" questions, like,

"What is a bastard?"

And we wax philosophic with metaphysical postulations, Incomplete aphorisms, and inconsistent sophisms that make one more and more sure that the only true thing is that a picture is worth a thousand words.

In the photo below, the guy on the right is a member of a bomb squad in the middle of a deactivation.

The guy behind him, well, he's a bastard.

OOOOH!

Late one dark night, two Nuns are riding their bicycles down the back streets of Rome trying to find their way back to the convent.

One leans over to the other and says,
"I've never come this way before."

The other nun blushes and whispers, "It's the cobblestones."

Thought For The Day:

Why don't sheep shrink when it rains?

Women like silent men; they think they're listening.

Men like Silence; they don't have to listen.

SON OF A BITCH FISH!

The parish priest went on a fishing trip.
On the last day of his trip he hooked a monster fish and proceeded to reel it in.

The guide, holding a net, yelled, "look at the size of that Son of a Bitch!"
"Son, I'm a priest. Your language is uncalled for!"

"No, Father, that's what kind of fish it is-a Son of a Bitch fish!"

"Really? Well then, help me land this Son of a Bitch!"

Once in the boat, they marvelled at the size of the monster.
"Father, that's the biggest Son of a Bitch I've ever seen."
"Yes, it is a big Son of a Bitch. What should I do with it?"
"Why, eat it of course. You've never tasted anything as good as Son of a Bitch!"

Elated, the priest headed home to the rectory.
While unloading his gear and his prize catch, Sister Mary inquired about his trip.
"Take a look at this big Son of a Bitch I caught!"
Sister Mary gasped and clutched her rosary; "Father!"
"It's OK, Sister. That's what kind of fish it is--a Son of a Bitch fish!"
"Oh, well then, what are you going to do with that big Son of a Bitch?"

"Why, eat it of course. The guide said nothing compares to the taste of a Son of a Bitch."

Sister Mary informed the priest that the new Bishop was scheduled to visit in a few days and that they should fix the Son of a Bitch for his dinner.

"I'll even clean the Son of a Bitch", she said.

As she was cleaning the huge fish, the Friar walked in.

"What are you doing Sister?"

"Father wants me to clean this big Son of a Bitch for the new Bishops' dinner."

"Sister! I'll clean it if you're so upset! Please watch your language!"

"No, no, no, it's called a Son of a Bitch fish."

"Really? Well, in that case, I'll fix up a great meal to go with it, and that Son of a Bitch can be the main course! Let me know when you've finished cleaning that Son of a Bitch."

On the night of the new Bishop's visit, everything was perfect.

The Friar had prepared an excellent meal. The wine was fine, and the fish was excellent.

The new Bishop said, "This is great fish, where did you get it?"

"I caught that Son of a Bitch!" proclaimed the proud priest.

The Bishop's eyes opened wide, but he said nothing.

"And I cleaned the Son of a Bitch!" exclaimed the Sister.

The Bishop sat silent in disbelief.

The Friar added, "And I prepared the Son of a Bitch, using a special recipe!"

The new Bishop looked around at each of them.

Slowly a big smile crept across his face as he said,

"You fuckers are my kind of people!!!

A Brilliant Genie?

A man walks up to a bar with an ostrich behind him, and as he sits a small cat jumps up on the stool beside him.

The bartender comes over, and asks for their order.

The man says, "I'll have a beer" and turns to the ostrich.

"What's yours?"

"I'll have a beer too" says the ostrich.

The cat says "I'll have a half beer, but I'm not paying for it".

The bartender pours the beer and says "That will be £6.40 please,"and the man reaches into his pocket and pulls out the exact change for payment.

This happens the next evening also.

The following evening the trio enters again.

"The usual?" asks thebartender.

"Well, its close to last call, so I'll have a large scotch", says the man, same for me" says the ostrich. "I'll have a small scotch, but I'm not paying for it" says the cat.

"That will be £12.35", says the bartender.

Once again the man pulls exact change out of his pocket and places it on the bar. The bartender can't hold back his curiosity any longer.

"Excuse me sir, How do you manage to always come up with the exact change out of your pocket every time" asks the bartender.

"Well," says the man, "several years ago I was cleaning the attic and found an old lamp. When I rubbed it, a Genie appeared and offered me 3 wishes. My first wish was that if I ever had to pay for anything, I just put my hand in my pocket, and the right amount of money would always be there."

"That's brilliant"! says the bartender, "Most people would wish for a million dollars or something, but you'll always be as rich as you want, for as long as you live."

"That's right!, Whether its a bottle of milk or a Rolls Royce, the exact money is always there" says the man.

The bartender asks, "One other thing sir, what's with the ostrich and the cat?"

The man replies, "Ah yes, they didn't work out quite so well; My other two wishes were for a chick with long legs and a tight pussy".

A BLONDE COP!

A blonde female police officer pulls over a blonde gal, in a convertible sports car, for speeding. She walks up to the car and asks the blond for her driver's license. The blonde convertible driver searches through her purse, in vain.
Finally she asks, "What does it look like?"

The blonde police officer tells her, "It's that thing with your picture on it."

The blonde driver searches for a few more seconds, pulls out her compact, opens it, and sure enough sees herself. She hands the compact to the blonde cop.

After a few seconds looking at the compact, the blonde cop rolls her eyes, hands the compact back to the blonde convertible driver and says, "If you had told me you were a police officer when I first pulled you over we could have avoided this whole thing."

~~~~~~~~~~~~~~~~~

Two fish are in a tank
One says to the other
"I'll man the guns, you drive"

A RISE?

I, the Penis hereby request a rise in salary for the following reasons:-
I do physical labour
I work at great depths
I plunge headfirst into everything I do
I do not get weekends off, nor public holidays
I work in a damp environment
I do not get paid overtime
I work in dark, poorly ventilated conditions
I work in high temperatures
My work exposes me to contagious diseases

MANAGEMENT RESPONSE:
Dear Penis,
After considering your request and assessing the arguments raised, the administration rejects your request for the following reasons:-
You do not work 8 hrs straight
You fall asleep on the job after brief work periods
You do not always follow the orders of the management team
You do not stay in your allocated position and often stray into other areas.
You do not take initiative and have to be pressured and stimulated to start working
You leave the worksite rather messy at the end of your shift
You often fail to observe necessary safety regulations, such as wearing the correct protective clothing
You will retire well before reaching 65
You are unable to work double shifts
You have been reported as regularly trying to get work elsewhere
You sometimes leave your allocated position before completing the job
And as if that were not all, you have been observed entering and leaving the workplace carrying two suspicious looking bags.

Sincerely,
The Management, Olympic Condoms!

The other day I phoned my local pizza
delivery firm and asked for a
thin and crusty supreme.
They sent me Diana Ross!

~~~~~~~~~~~~~~~~~~~~~~~~~~~~~~~~~~~~~

No More Children

After having their 11th child, an Irish couple decided that was
enough, as they could not afford a larger bed. So the husband went
to his doctor and told him that he and his wife didn't want to have
any more children. The doctor told him that there was a procedure
called a vasectomy that could fix the problem but that it was
expensive. A less costly alternative, said the doctor, was to go home,
get a firecracker, light it, put it in a beer can, then hold the can up to
his ear and count to 10. The Irishman said to the doctor, "I may not
be the smartest man in the world, but I don't see how putting a
firecracker in a beer can next to my ear is going to help me."
"Trust me," said the doctor. So the man went home, lit a firecracker
and put it in a beer can. He held the can up to his ear and began to
count: "1" "2" "3" "4" "5" at which point he paused, placed the beer
can between his legs, and resumed counting on his other hand.

<u>DAVIDS PARROT</u>

David received a parrot for his birthday. The parrot was fully grown with a bad attitude and worse vocabulary. Every other word was an expletive.

Those that weren't expletives, were to say the least, rude. David tried hard to change the bird's attitude and was constantly saying polite words, playing soft music, anything he could think of to try and set a good example... Nothing worked.
He yelled at the bird and the bird yelled back.
He shook the bird and the bird just got angrier and ruder. Finally, in a moment of desperation, David put the parrot in the freezer. For a few moments he heard the bird squawk and kick and scream-then suddenly, there was quiet. Not a sound for half a minute. David was frightened that he might have hurt the bird and quickly opened the freezer door. The parrot calmly stepped out onto David's extended arm and said, "I believe I may have offended you with my rude language and actions. I will endeavour at once to correct my behaviour. I really am truly sorry and beg your forgiveness." David was astonished at the bird's change in attitude and was about to ask what had made such a dramatic change when the parrot continued, "May I ask what the chicken did?"

~~~~~~~~~~~~~~~~~~~~

Give a man a fish and he will eat for a day.
Teach him how to fish, and he will sit in a boat
and drink beer all day

BE CAREFUL WHERE YOU SIT

A lady about 8 months pregnant got on a bus. She noticed the man opposite her was smiling at her. She immediately moved to another seat.

This time the smile turned into a grin, so she moved again. The man seemed more amused. When on the fourth move, the man burst out laughing, she complained to the driver and he had the man arrested.

The case came up in court. The judge asked the man (about 20 years old) what he had to say for himself. The man replied, "Well your Honour, it was like this:

When the lady got on the bus, I couldn't help but notice her condition.

She sat under a sweets sign that said, "The Double Mint Twins are Coming and I grinned.
Then she moved and sat under a sign that said,
"Logan's Liniment will reduce the swelling", and I had to smile.
Then she placed herself under a deodorant sign that said, "William's Big Stick Did the Trick", and I could hardly contain myself.

BUT, your Honour, when she moved the fourth time and sat under a sign that said, "Goodyear Rubber could have prevented this Accident"... I just lost it."

"CASE DISMISSED!!"

~~~~~~~~~~~~~~~~~~~~~~~~~~

Why don't cannibals eat clowns?
Because they taste funny

Thought For The Day:

If the No. 2 pencil is the most popular,

why is it still No.2?

~~~~~~~~~~~~~~~~~~~~~~~~~~

SkyTV have just won the rights to screen the first World Origami Championships from Tokyo.

Unfortunately it's only available on Paper View...

__Not So Smart?__

A Jelly Baby walks into a bar and starts talking to a Smartie. After a few beers the Smartie says "Ere, a bunch of us are heading to that new club, fancy tagging along?" The Jelly Baby says "No mate, I'm a soft centre, I always end up getting my head kicked in." So Smartie says "Don't worry about it, I'm a bit of a hard case, I'll look after you."

Jelly Baby thinks about it for a minute and says "Fair enough, as long as you'll look after me", and off they go.
After a few more beers in the club, three Lockets walk in. As soon as he sees them, Smartie hides under the table. The Lockets take one look at Jelly Baby and start kicking him, breaking bottles over his little jelly head, lamping him with little sugary chairs, and generally having a laugh. After a while they get bored and walk out.

Jelly Baby pulls his battered Jelly Baby body over to the table and wipes up his Jelly Baby blood and turns to Smartie and says "I thought you were going to look after me."

"I was!" says Smartie, "But those Lockets are f...ing menthol....

~~~~~~~~~~~~~~~~~~~~~~~

Did You Know?

$$111,111,111 \times 111,111,111 = 12,345,678,987,654,321$$

Bet you're reaching for that calculator now eh?

HOW TO TELL THE SEX OF A FLY!!

A woman walked into the kitchen to find her husband stalking around with a fly swatter.

"What are you doing?" she asked.

"Hunting Flies" he responded.

"Oh. Killing any?" she asked.

"Yep, 3 males and 2 females," he replied.

Intrigued, she asked, "How can you tell?"

He responded, "3 were on a beer can and 2 were on the phone".

SORRY - HEAVEN IS FULL TODAY

Three men were standing in line to get into heaven one day. It had been a pretty busy day, so Peter had to tell the first one, "Heaven's getting pretty close to full today, and I've been asked to admit only people who have had particularly horrible deaths. So what's your story?"

So the first man replies: "Well, for a while I've suspected my wife has been cheating on me, so today I came home early to try to catch her red-handed. As I came into my 25th floor apartment, I could tell something was wrong, but all my searching around didn't reveal where this other guy could have been hiding.
Finally, I went out to the balcony, and sure enough, there was this man hanging off the railing, 25 floors above ground! I was really mad, so I started beating on him, but he wouldn't fall off.
So finally I got a hammer and starting hammering on his fingers. Of course, he couldn't stand that for long, so he let go and fell -- but even after 25 stories, he fell into the bushes, stunned but okay.
I couldn't stand it anymore, so I ran into the kitchen, grabbed the fridge and threw it over the edge where it landed on him, killing him instantly.
But all the stress and anger got to me, and I had a heart attack and died there on the balcony."
"That sounds like a pretty bad day to me," said Peter, and let the man in.

The second man comes up and Peter explains to him about heaven being full, and again asks for his story.
"It's been a very strange day. You see, I live on the 26th floor of my apartment building, and every morning I do my exercises out on my balcony.
Well, this morning I must have slipped or something, because I fell over the edge. But I got lucky, and caught the railing of the balcony on the floor below me.
I knew I couldn't hang on for very long, when suddenly this man burst out onto the balcony. I thought for sure I was saved, but he started beating me. I held on the best I could until he grabbed a hammer and started pounding on my hands. Finally I just let go, but again I got lucky and fell into the bushes below, stunned but all right. Just when I was thinking I was going to be okay, this refrigerator comes falling out of the sky and crushes me instantly, and now I'm here."

Once again, Peter had to concede that that sounded like a pretty horrible death.

The third man came to the front of the line, and again Peter explained that heaven was full and asked for his story.

"Picture this," says the third man, "I'm hiding naked inside a refrigerator..."

Who Can Ring My Bell?

Twelve priests were about to be ordained. The final test was for them to line up in a straight row, totally nude, in a garden while a sexy and beautiful, big breasted, nude model danced before them. Each priest had a small bell attached to his penis and they were told that anyone whose bell rang when she danced in front of them would not be ordained because he had not reached a state of spiritual purity.

The beautiful model danced before the first candidate, with no reaction.

She proceeded down the line with the same response from all the priests until she got to the final priest.

As she danced, his bell began to ring so loudly that it flew off and fell clattering to the ground.

Embarrassed, the priest took a few steps forward, bent over to pick it up...........

and suddenly all the other bells rang loudly!

~~~~~~

Curse

An old man goes to the Wizard to ask him if he can remove a "Curse" he has been living with for many years.

The Wizard says "Maybe, but you will have to tell me the exact words that were used to put the curse on you."

The old man says without hesitation,

"I now pronounce you man and wife."

RECEPTIONISTS

There's nothing worse than a snotty doctor's receptionist who insists you tell her what is wrong in a room full of other patients. I know most of us have experienced this. You have got to love the way this old guy handled it.

A 86 year old man walked into a crowded doctor's waiting room. As he approached the desk, the receptionist said, "Yes sir, what are you seeing the doctor for today?" "There's something wrong with my dick," he replied.
The receptionist became irritated and said "You shouldn't come into a crowded office and say things like that."
"Why not? You asked me what was wrong and I told you," he said.
The receptionist replied, "You've obviously caused some embarrassment in this room full of people.
You should have said there is something wrong with your ear or something and then discussed the problem further with the doctor in private.
"The man replied, "You shouldn't ask people things in a room full of others, if the answer could embarrass anyone."

The man walked out, waited several minutes and then re-entered.
The receptionist smiled smugly and asked, "Yes?"
"There's something wrong with my ear," he stated.
The receptionist nodded approvingly and smiled, knowing he had taken her advice. "And what is wrong with your ear, Sir?"
"I can't piss out of it," the man replied.

The waiting room erupted in laughter!

BAG OF LOLLIES SON?

One day a 12 year old boy was walking down the street when a car pulled up beside him and the driver wound down the window.
"I'll give you a bag of lollies if you get in the car" , said the driver.
"No way, get stuffed" replied the boy.

"How about a bag of lollies and £10. the driver asked.
"no way" replied the boy.

"What about a bag of lollies and £50?" asked the driver."No, I'm not getting in the car" answered the boy.

"Okay, I'll give you a bag of lollies and £100" the driver offered."No!" replied the boy."
"What will it take to get you in the car?" asked the driver.

The boy replied "Listen Dad. you bought the bloody Volvo, you live with it".

FANCY DRESS PARTY

A couple was invited to a swanky family masked fancy dress Halloween party.

The wife got a terrible headache and told her husband to go to the party alone. He, being a devoted husband, protested, but she argued and said she was going to take some aspirin and go to bed, and there was no need for his good time to be spoiled by not going. So he took his costume and away he went.

The wife, after sleeping soundly for about an hour, awakened without pain, and, as it was still early, decided to go to the party. In as much as her husband did not know what her costume was, she thought she would have some fun by watching her husband to see how he acted when she was not with him. So she joined the party and soon spotted her husband cavorting around on the dance floor, dancing with every nice chick he could and copping a little feel here and a little kiss there. His wife went up to him and being a rather seductive babe herself, he left his partner high and dry and devoted his time to the new stuff that had just arrived.

She let him go as far as he wished, naturally, since he was her husband.

After some more to drink he finally whispered a little proposition in her ear and she agreed, so off they went to one of the cars and had a quickie in the back seat.

Just before unmasking at midnight, she slipped away and went home and put the costume away and got into bed, wondering what kind of explanation he would make up for his outrageous behaviour. She was sitting up reading when he came in, so she asked what kind of time he had.

He said, "Oh, the same old thing. You know I never have a good time when you're not there."

Then she asked, "Did you dance much?"

He replied, "I'll tell you, I never even danced one dance. When I got there, I met Pete, Bill Brown and some other guys, so we went into the spare room and played poker all evening."

Then she said with unashamed sarcasm, "You must have looked really silly wearing that costume playing poker all night!"

And the husband returned "actually I gave my costume to your Dad and apparently he had a whale of a time"

Nursery Rhymes?

Mary had a little skirt
With splits right up the sides
Every time that Mary walked
The boys could see her Thighs
Mary had another skirt
T'was given to her by her Granny
...but she didn't wear that one very often

Mary had a little lamb
Her father shot it dead.
Now it goes to school with her,
between two chunks of bread.

Mary had a little lamb
It ran into a pylon.
10,000 volts went up it's ass
and turned it's wool to nylon

Jack and Jill
Went up the hill
to have some hanky panky.
Silly Jill forgot her pill
And now there's little Franky.

WALES

Two tourists were driving through Wales.

As they were approaching Llanfairpwllgwyngyllgogerychwyrndrobwllllantysiliogogogoch, they started arguing about the pronunciation of the town's name.

They argued back and forth until they stopped for lunch.

As they stood at the counter one tourist asked the blonde employee, "Before we order, could you please settle an argument for us?

Would you please pronounce where we are ... very slowly?

The girl leaned over the counter and said,

"Burrrrrrr, Gerrrrrrr,Kiiiiiing.

~~~~~~~~~~~~~~~~~~~~~~~~~~~~~~~~~~~~

Change is inevitable, except from a vending machine

THINGS WE HAVE LEARNED FROM THE MOVIES

The ventilation system of any building is the perfect hiding place. No one will ever think of looking for you in there and you can travel to any other part of the building you want without difficulty.

When paying for a taxi, don't look at your wallet as you take out a bill - just grab one at random and hand it over. It will always be the exact fare.

Kitchens don't have light switches. When entering a kitchen at night, you should open the fridge door and use that light instead.

Television news bulletins usually contain a story that affects you personally at that precise moment.

A single match will be sufficient to light up a room the size of Wembley Stadium.

It is always possible to park directly outside the building you are visiting.

THE WRONG CONCLUSION

A young couple about to be married were looking at a house in the country. After satisfying themselves it was suitable, they went home. During the journey home the young lady was thoughtful, and when asked why, replied "did you notice where the W.C. was Charles?" He replied, no he had not, so when they arrived back he wrote to the landlord asking where it was situated. The landlord being ignorant did not understand the term W.C. and came to the conclusion it meant the Weslyan Chapel, and he answered as follows.

Dear Sir
I have great pleasure to inform you that the W.C. is situated about nine miles from the house, and is capable of holding 200 people. This is an unfortunate situation if you are in the habit of going regularly, but you will be glad to know, that a great number of people take their lunch and make a day of it, whilst others who can camp and spare the time, go by car and arrive in the nick of time. It will be interesting for you to know that my daughter was married in the W.C. in fact it was there she first met her husband. I remember the day of the wedding on account of the rush for seats, and the splendid reports we heard afterwards. There were 10 people on a seat usually occupied by two. It was wonderful to see the expressions on their faces.
My brothers were there too for they have gone regularly since they were christened.
A bazaar is to be held next to the W.C. and the proceeds are going to help provide tip-up seats, as members have felt that this is a long felt want. My wife and I are getting older now, and do not go as often as we used to. It is six years since we last went. I assure you it hurts us very much, not being able to go more regularly.

Yours Faithfully

P.S. There are hymn sheets behind the door.
Please replace them after use! "Thank You"

The Road to Enlightenment !

(The Teachings of Zen?)

1. Do not walk behind me, for I may not always lead. Do not walk ahead of me, for I may not always follow. Do not walk beside me for the path is narrow. In fact, go away and find your own place to walk.

2. The journey of a thousand miles begins with a broken fan belt and a flat tyre.

3. The darkest hour is just before dawn. So if you're going to steal your neighbour's milk, that's the time to do it.

4. Sex is like air. It's not important unless you aren't getting any.

5. Don't be irreplaceable. If you can't be replaced, you can't be promoted.

6. No one is listening until you f*rt.

7. Never test the depth of the water with both feet.

8. Before you criticise someone, you should walk a mile in their shoes. That way, when you criticise them, you're a mile away and you have their shoes.

10. If at first you don't succeed, skydiving is not for you.

11. Some days you are the fly; some days you are the windscreen.

12. Don't worry; it only seems kinky the first time.

13. Good judgement comes from bad experience, and a lot of that comes from bad judgement.

14. The quickest way to double your money is to fold it in half and put it back in your pocket.

15. There are two theories to arguing with women. Neither one works.

WOMEN HAVE WAYS WITH WORDS

A sulky teenage boy comes down to breakfast. Since they live on a farm, his mother asks if he had done his chores. "Not yet," said the lad. His mother tells him no breakfast until he does his chores.

Well, he's a little pissed, so he goes to feed the chickens, and he kicks a chicken. He goes to feed the cows, and he kicks a cow. He goes to feed the pigs, and he kicks a pig.

He goes back in for breakfast and his mother gives him a bowl of dry cereal.
"How come I don't get any eggs and bacon? Why don't I have any milk in my cereal?" he grunts.

"Well," his mother says, "I saw you kick a chicken, so you don't get any eggs for a week. I saw you kick the pig, so you don't get any bacon for a week either. I also saw you kick the cow, so for a week you aren't getting any milk."

Just then, his father comes down for breakfast and kicks the cat half way across the kitchen. The lad looks up at his mother with a smile, and says, "Are you going to tell him, or should I?"

~~~~~~

Generally speaking, you aren't learning much when your lips are moving

What a woman says:

"This place is a mess! C'mon! You and I need to clean up! Your stuff is lying on the floor and you'll have no clothes to wear if we don't do laundry right now! "

What a man hears:

"blah,blah,blah,blah,
C'MON blah,blah,blah,blah,
YOU AND I blah, blah,blah,blah,
ON THE FLOOR blah,blah,blah,blah,
NO CLOTHES blah,blah,blah,blah,
RIGHT NOW "

~~~~~~~~~~~~~~~~~~~~~~~~~~~~~~~~~~~~~

BRUNETTE?

A young brunette goes into the doctor's office and says that her body hurts wherever she touches it.
"Impossible," says the doctor. "Show me."
She takes her finger and pushes her elbow and screams in agony.
She pushes her knee and screams, pushes her ankle and screams.
Everywhere she touches makes her scream.
The doctor says, "You're not really a brunette, are you?"
She says "No, I'm really a blonde".
"I thought so," he says. "You have a broken finger."

SKUNK AROMA

A married couple are driving along when they see a wounded skunk on the side of the road. They stop, the wife gets out, picks it up, and brings it into the car. She says, "Look, it's shivering, it must be cold. What should I do?" Her husband replies, "Put it between your legs to keep it warm." She asks, "What about the smell?" He says, "Hold its nose."

~~~~~~~~~~~~~~~~~~~~~~~~~~~~~~~~~~~~~~~

BE FIRM

One morning while she was making breakfast, the local fitness freak walked up to his wife, pinched her on the bum and said, "You know dear if you firmed this up we could get rid of your girdles." This was a bit over the limit, but she controlled herself and replied with silence. Next morning the man woke his wife with a pinch on the breast. "You know love if you firmed these up we could get rid of your bras." That was too far over the limit. She rolled over and grabbed him by the penis. Maintaining a vice grip she whispered in ear, "You know dear if you firmed this up we could get rid of the gardener, the pool man and your brother."

DON'T SWING!

Toward the end of the golf course, Dave somehow managed to hit his ball into the woods finding it in a patch of pretty yellow buttercups. Trying to get his ball back in play, he ended up thrashing just about every buttercup in the patch.
All of a sudden . . . POOF! In a flash and puff of smoke, a little old woman appeared. She said, "I'm Mother Nature! Do you know how long it took me to make those buttercups? Just for that, you won't have any butter for your popcorn the rest of your life; better still; you won't have any butter for your toast for the rest of your life... as a matter of fact, you won't have any butter for anything the rest of your life!"
THEN POOF! She was gone.
After Dave got hold of himself, he hollered for his friend, Steve. "Steve, where are you?"
Steve yells back, "I'm over here, in the pussy willows."
Dave yells back... "DON'T SWING, STEVE!!! For the love of God, DON'T SWING!!!"

~~~~~~

NEW FLAT!!

Following a night out with a few friends, a man brought them back to show off his new flat. After the grand tour, the visitors were rather perplexed by the large gong taking pride of place in the lounge.

"What's that big brass gong for?" one of the guests asked.
"Why, that's my Speaking Clock" the man replied.
"How does it work?"
"I'll show you", the man said, giving the gong an ear-shattering blow with an unpadded hammer.
Suddenly, a voice from the other side of the wall screamed, "For Christs sake, it's twenty to two in the ****ing morning!!"

The Hatpin

A man goes up to the minister at the local church.

"Reverend," he said, "we have a problem. My wife keeps falling asleep during your sermons. It's very embarrassing, not to mention disrespectful. What should I do?"
"I've noticed this and have an idea if you're up to the task," said the minister. "Take this hatpin with you. I will be able to tell when Mrs. Jones is sleeping, and I will motion to you at specific times. When I motion, you give her a good poke in the leg."

In church the following Sunday, Mrs. Jones dozed off. Noticing this, the preacher put his plan to "And who made the ultimate sacrifice for you?" he said, nodding to Mr. Jones.
"Jesus!" Mrs. Jones cried out as her husband jabbed her in the leg with the sharp object.
"Yes! You are correct, Mrs. Jones!" came the minister's quick reply.

Soon, Mrs. Jones nodded off again. And again, the minister noticed. Who is your Redeemer?" he asked the congregation, motioning toward Mr. Jones.
"My God!" howled Mrs. Jones as she was stuck again with the pin.
"Right again!" bellowed the minister, a slight grin on his face.

Before long, Mrs. Jones again winked off. However, this time the minister did not notice. As he picked up the tempo of his sermon, he made a few hand gestures that Mr. Jones mistook as signals to bayonet his wife with the hatpin yet again.

The minister asked, "And what did Eve say to Adam after she bore him his 99th son?" As Mr. Jones enthusiastically poked his wife's thigh with the hatpin piercing her skin she screamed:
"You stick that f***ing thing in me one more time and I'll break it in half and shove it up your arse!"
"Amen!" replied all the women in the congregation.

The Rope

There were 11 people hanging onto a rope attached to a helicopter.

Ten men and one woman.

They all decided that one person should get off because if they didn't the rope would break and everyone would die.
They couldn't decide who should go, so finally the woman gave a really touching speech saying how she would give up her life to save the others, because women were used to giving up things for their husbands and children, giving in to men, and not receiving anything in return.

When she finished speaking, all the men clapped.

Never underestimate the power of a Woman!

~~~~~~

HANKY PANKY?

A man and a woman who have never met before find themselves in the same sleeping carriage of a train. After the initial embarrassment, they both go to sleep, the woman on the top bunk, the man on the lower. In the middle of the night the woman leans over, wakes the man and says, "I'm sorry to bother you, but I'm awfully cold and I was wondering if you could possibly get me another blanket."
The man leans out and, with a glint in his eye, says,
"I've got a better idea. Just for tonight, let's pretend we're married"
The woman thinks for a moment. "Why not?", she giggles, in anticipation.
"Great!" He replies, "Get your own f***ing blanket!"

MORE THINGS WE HAVE LEARNED FROM THE MOVIES

A detective can only solve a case once he has been suspended from duty.

It does not matter if you are heavily outnumbered in a fight involving martial arts - your enemies will wait patiently to attack you one by one by dancing around in a threatening manner until you have knocked out their predecessors.

Police Departments give their officers personality tests to make sure they are deliberately assigned a partner who is their total opposite.

An electric fence powerful enough to kill a dinosaur will cause no lasting damage to an eight-year-old child.

If staying in a haunted house, women should investigate any strange noises in their most revealing underwear.

It is not necessary to say hello or goodbye when beginning or ending phone conversations.

"THE RUMOR"

The Texas preacher rose with an angry red face. "Someone in this congregation has spread a rumor that I belong to the Ku Klux Klan. This is a horrible lie and one which a Christian community cannot tolerate. I am embarrassed and do not intend to accept this.

Now, I want the party who did this to stand and ask forgiveness from God and this Christian family." No one moved.

The preacher continued, "Do you have the nerve to face me and admit this is a falsehood? Remember, you will be forgiven and in your heart you will feel glory. Now stand and confess your transgression." Again all was quiet.

Then, slowly, a drop-dead gorgeous blonde with a body that would stop traffic rose from the third pew. Her head was bowed and her voice quivered as she spoke. "Reverend there has been a terrible misunderstanding. I never said you were a member of the Klan. I simply told a couple of my friends that you were a wizard under the sheets!"

The preacher fainted.

~~~~~~~~~~~~~~~~~~~~~~~~~~~

Bikini or All-in-One?

While shopping for vacation clothes, my husband and I passed a display of bathing suits. It had been at least ten years and twenty pounds since I had even considered buying a bathing suit, so I sought my husband's advice.
"What do you think?" I asked. "Should I get a bikini or an all-in-one?"
"Better get a bikini," he replied. "You'd never get it all in one."

Sayings For The Less Than Talented:

Not the sharpest knife in the drawer.

A few clowns short of a circus.

A few Cokes short of a six-pack.

A few peas short of a casserole.

The wheel's spinning, but the hamster's dead.

All froth and no beer.

The cheese slid off his cracker.

Her sewing machine's out of thread.

His belt doesn't go through all the loops.

Not enough grain in the silo.

Proof that evolution CAN go in reverse.

In the pinball game of life, his flippers were a little further apart than most.

A Lot Of Kids

Maria, an Italian woman was extremely religious. When she was married, she refused to use protection because she felt that birth control was going against God's will. She and her husband had seventeen kids.

Maria's husband got sick and passed away. As time went by, Maria moved on with her life and married another man. Again, she refused to use protection because of her religious beliefs. She and her second husband had fifteen kids.

Again, Maria lost her husband. But, soon after her husband's death, she passed away as well. At the ceremony at the cemetery the priest looked down at the coffin then looked up at the sky and said, "They're finally together."

This confuses one of the family members at the service and after the ceremony, asks the priest. "Father," he starts, "back at the cemetery when you said, 'they're finally together,' did you mean Maria and her first husband, or Maria and her second husband?"

The father takes a long look at him and says, "I was talking about her legs."

~~~~~~~~~~~~~~~~~~~~~~~~~~~~

TIGHT PANTS

This guy has been sitting in a bar all night, staring at a blonde wearing the tightest pants he's ever seen. Finally his curiosity gets the best of him, so he walks over and asks, "How do you get into those pants?"
The young woman looks him over and replies, "Well, you could start by buying me a drink."

WHERE ARE ALL THE DIPSTICKS?

There are a lot of folks who can't understand how we came to have an oil shortage here in America.

Well, there's a very simple answer......Nobody bothered to check the oil.
We just didn't know we were getting low.
The reason for that is purely geographical.

All our oil is in Alaska, Texas, California, and Oklahoma.

All our dipsticks are in Washington, DC

~~~~~~~~~~~~~~~~~~~~~~~~~~~~~~~~~~

Sexual Harassment

A man walks up to a woman in his office each day, stands very close to her, draws in a large breath of air and tells her that her hair smells nice.

After a week of this, she can't stand it any longer, and goes to Human Resources. Without identifying the guy, she tells them what the co-worker does, and that she wants to file a sexual harassment suit against him.

The HR supervisor is puzzled by this approach, and asks, "What's sexually threatening about a co-worker telling you your hair smells nice?"

The woman replies, "Its Keith, the midget".

THINGS YOU'D LOVE TO SAY AT WORK

I thought I wanted a career, turns out I just wanted paycheques

I have plenty of talent and vision. I just don't give a damn.

I like you. You remind me of when I was young and stupid.

It sounds like English, but I can't understand a word you're saying (Marketing Strategy Meeting)

I'm out of my mind, but feel free to leave a message...

I'll try being nicer if you'll try being smarter.

Hmm, yes, I can see your point, and it's such a shame that you're wrong.

How about never? Is never good for you?

Two Aliens

Two aliens landed in the West Texas desert near an abandoned gas station.

They approached one of the gas pumps, and one of the aliens addressed it.

"Greetings, earthling. We come in peace. Take us to your leader."

The gas pump, of course, didn't respond. The alien repeated the greeting. There was no response. The alien annoyed by what he perceived to be the gas pump's haughty attitude, drew his ray gun, and said impatiently, "Greetings, earthling. We come in peace. How dare you ignore us in this way! Take us to your leader, or I'll fire!"

The other alien shouted to his comrade "No, you don't want to make him mad!" But before he finished his warning, the first alien fired. There was a huge explosion that blew both of them 200 meters into the desert, where they landed in a heap. When they finally regained consciousness, the one who fired turned to the other one and said, "What a ferocious creature. It damn near killed us! How did you know it was so dangerous?"

The other alien answered "If there's one thing I've learned during my travels through the galaxy ... Any guy who can wrap his penis around himself twice and then stick it in his own ear, is someone you shouldn't mess with."

He Said…She Said……

He said … I don't know why you wear a bra; you've got nothing to put in it.
She said … You wear pants don't you?

He said … Since I first laid eyes on you, I've wanted to make love to you really badly.
She said … Well, you succeeded!

He said … Shall we try swapping positions tonight?
She said … That's a good idea - you stand by the ironing board while I sit on the sofa and fart!

He said … What have you been doing with all the grocery money I gave you?
She said … Turn sideways and look in the mirror!

He said … Why don't you tell me when you have an orgasm?
She said … I would but you're never there.

On a wall in a ladies room … "My husband follows me everywhere"
Written just below it … " I do not"

HOW TO SPEAK ABOUT MEN AND BE POLITICALLY CORRECT:

1. He does not have a BEER GUT - He has developed a LIQUID STORAGE FACILITY.

2. He is not a BAD DANCER - He is OVERLY CAUCASIAN.

3. He does not GET LOST - He INVESTIGATES ALTERNATIVE DESTINATIONS.

4. He is not BALDING - He is in FOLLICLE REGRESSION.

5. He is not a CRADLE SNATCHER - He is GENERATIONALLY DIFFERENTIAL.

6. He does not get FALLING-DOWN DRUNK - He becomes ACCIDENTALLY HORIZONTAL.

7. He does not act like a TOTAL ASS - He develops RECTAL CRANIAL INVERSION.

8. He is not a MALE CHAUVINIST PIG - He has SWINE EMPATHY.

9. He is not afraid of COMMITMENT - He is MONOGAMOUSLY CHALLENGED.

Save the best till last..........

10. He is not a WAN*ER - He is an OWNER OPERATOR.

EXTRA LARGE CONDOMS

A woman walks into a drugstore and asks the pharmacist if he sells extra large condoms.
He replies, "Yes we do. Would you like to buy some?"
She responds, "No sir, but do you mind if I wait around here until someone does?"

~~~~~~~~~~~~~~~~~~~

WHAT ARE WE EATING DAD?

A hunter kills a deer and brings it home. He decides to clean and serve the venison for supper. He knows his kids are fussy eaters, and won't eat it if they know what it is - so he does not tell them.
His little son, Jimmy, keeps asking him, "What's for supper?"
"You'll see", says his dad.
They start eating supper and his daughter, Katie, keeps asking what they're eating. "Ok," says her Dad, "here's a hint, its what your mother sometimes calls me."
His daughter, Katie, screams... "Don't eat it Jimmy, its an asshole!"

EXCUSE ME SIR......

A man in his 40s bought a new BMW and was out driving on the M11 at top speed when he suddenly saw flashing blue lights behind him.
 'There's no way they can catch a BMW,' he thought to himself and sped up even more. Then the reality of the situation hit him, 'What the hell am I doing?' he thought and pulled over.
 The traffic cop came up to him, took his driving license without a word, and examined it and the car. 'It's been a long day, it is the end of my shift, and it's Friday the 13th. I don't feel like more paperwork, so if you can
 give me an excuse for your driving that I haven't heard before, you can go.'
 The man thinks for a second and says, 'Last week my wife ran off with a policeman. I was afraid you were trying to give her back.'

'Have a nice weekend,' said the officer.

~~~~~~~~~~~~~~~~~~~~

COAST GUARD

A married couple were asleep when the phone rang at 2 in the morning.
The wife (undoubtedly blonde), picked up the phone, listened a moment and said, "How should I know, that's 200 miles from here!" and hung up.
The husband said, "Who was that?"
The wife said, "I don't know; some woman wanting to know if the coast is clear."

THE PARROT

Mrs. Davidson's dishwasher quit working, so she called a repairman. He couldn't accommodate her with an evening appointment. Since she had to go to work the next day, she told him: "I'll leave the key under the mat. "Fix the dishwasher, leave the bill on the counter, and I'll mail you the cheque. By the way, don't worry about my Doberman. He won't bother you. But, whatever you do, ...do NOT under any circumstances talk to my parrot!"

When the repairman arrived at Mrs. Davidson's apartment the next day, he discovered the biggest and meanest looking Doberman he had ever seen.
But, just as she had said, the dog just lay there on the carpet, watching the repairman go about his business. However, the whole time he was there, the parrot drove him nuts with its incessant yelling, cursing, and name-calling.
Finally the repairman couldn't contain himself any longer and yelled:
"Shut up, you stupid ugly bird!"

To which the parrot replied:
"Get him Spike!"

PADDY & MURPHY GO SHOPPING

2 Irishmen in London whilst looking for work were strolling down Oxford Street. After walking for a few minutes, Paddy turns to Murphy with a look of amazement on his face and says: "Murphy, will you have a look at that shop over there, I thought that London was supposed to be expensive but that shop is as cheap as chips."

Murphy says: "Paddy you're right so you are, will you have a look at That.

Suits £10.00, Shirts £4.00, Trousers £5.00, I think that we should buy a job lot and take them back to Ireland. We would make a tidy Profit selling them in Dublin so we would." Paddy says in agreement: "Murphy that is as good an idea as you'll ever have, but I'm pretty sure that you have to pay taxes and duty on things like that. The shopkeeper will never let us have them if he thinks that we're gonna export them and make our fortune, so he won't."

Murphy thinks and says: "Paddy, I've got idea! You can do the best English accent out of the pair of us. You go in there and do the Talking and I'll just stand behind you and say nothing. He'll never guess we're Irish so he won't."

"OK Murphy", agrees Paddy, "I'll do the talking, you just stand there and look English."

So the two visitors to our illustrious capital city go into the shop, where Paddy is greeted politely by the owner. Paddy then proceeds to do his best Phil Mitchell impression; "Awwwight Guvnor, I'll 'ave 20 of yer 'Whistle 'un Flutes', 20 'Dickie Dirts' and 20 pairs of strides. And if yer don't mind I'll be paying with the 380 'Pictures of the Queen' in my 'Sky Rocket'."

Upon hearing this request from Paddy, the owner smiles, takes a look at Murphy as well then asks Paddy ...

"You're Irish aren't you?"

Quite bemused, Paddy replies, "Oh be'Jasus. Mary mother of Christ, if that isn't me best English accent. How in God's name did you know that we were Irish?"

The Owner replies. "This is a Dry Cleaners mate"

IRISH WORKING GIRL

An Irish girl went to London to work as a secretary and began sending home money and gifts to her parents. After a few years they asked her to come home for a visit, as her father was getting frail and elderly.

She pulled up to the family home in a Rolls Royce and stepped out wearing furs and diamonds. As she walked into the house her father said, "Hmmm -they seem to be paying secretaries awfully well in London."

The girl took his hands and said "Da - I've been meaning to tell you something for years but I didn't want to put it in a letter. I can't hide it from you any longer. I've become a prostitute."

Her father gasped, put his hand on his heart and keeled over. The doctor was called but the old man had clearly lost the will to live. He was put to bed and the family called the priest too.

As the priest began to administer Extreme Unction, with the mother and daughter weeping and wailing, the old man muttered weakly "I'm a goner- killed by my own daughter! Killed by the shame of what you've become!"

"Please forgive me," his daughter sobbed, "I only wanted to have nice things! I wanted to be able to send you money and the only way I could do it was by becoming a prostitute.

Brushing the priest aside, the old man sat bolt upright in bed, smiling. "Did you say prostitute? I thought you said Protestant!"

CLEVER COP?

A city cop was on his horse waiting to cross the street when a little girl named Mary stopped beside him on her new shiny bike.

"Nice bike" the cop said "did Santa bring it to you?"

"Yep," the little girl said, "he sure did!"

The cop looked the bike over and handed the girl a $20 ticket for a safety violation, saying "Next year tell Santa to put a reflector light on the back of it."

The young girl looked up at the cop and said, "Nice horse you got there sir, did Santa bring it to you?"

"Yes, he sure did," chuckled the cop.

The little girl looked up at the cop and said, "Next year tell Santa the dick goes underneath the horse, not on top."

~~~~~~~~~~~~~~~~~~~~~~~~~

How Clever are You?

Q. If you were to spell out numbers, how far would you have to go until you would find the letter "A"?

A. One thousand

RUBBER MAN

John goes for a job in the Quality Assurance department at Durex.
The foreman takes him round the plant and shows him all the
machinery and offers him the job.
"What will the role entail exactly?" Asks the man.

"Well", says the foreman, "you have to check one in a hundred", and
proceeds to remove one of the rubbers from the production line,
stretches it, holds it up to the lights, then places it over his
manhood, then calls the secretary over. She proceeds to hitch her
skirt up, pull her knickers down and bends over. The foreman does
the business and after he's finished he removes the Durex, stretches
it, holds it up to the light again to confirm no holes.

"Easy as that", he says.

"When do I start?" Asks the man, unable to believe his luck.
"Monday, 8:00 sharp!"

Naturally, our hero hardly sleeps a wink all Sunday night, and is
outside the Durex factory waiting to get in at 6:30.
Anyway, the production line starts up and the man faithfully counts
out 100 ribbed black mambo's (lubricated with ensodol for extra
comfort). He picks up the 101st, stretches it, holds it up to the light
to check for holes then pulls it over his manhood and calls the
secretary over.

Over she comes, grabs hold of his manhood, and proceeds to
vigorously masturbate him. Rather startled and confused, the man
just looks at the secretary who says...........

"Sorry, it's company policy. You've got to work a week in hand"

IRISH MEDICAL DICTIONARY:

Artery..........................The study of paintings
Bacteria........................Back door to cafeteria
Barium.........................What doctors do when patients die
Benign.........................What you be, after you be eight
Caesarean Section...............A neighbourhood in Rome
Catscan.........................Searching for Kitty
Cauterize.......................Made eye contact with her
Colic...........................A sheep dog
Coma...........................A punctuation mark
Dilate..........................To live long
Enema..........................Not a friend
Fester..........................Quicker than someone else
Fibula..........................A small lie
Impotent.......................Distinguished, well known
Labour Pain.....................Getting hurt at work
Medical Staff...................A Doctor's cane
Morbid.........................A higher offer
Nitrates........................Cheaper than day rates
Node...........................I knew it
Outpatient......................A person who has fainted
Pelvis..........................Second cousin to Elvis
Post Operative..................A letter carrier
Recovery Room..................Place to do upholstery
Rectum.........................Nearly killed him
Secretion.......................Hiding something
Seizure.........................Roman emperor
Tablet..........................A small table
Terminal Illness.................Getting sick at the airport
Tumour.........................One plus one more
Urine...........................Opposite of you're out

EVEN MORE THINGS WE HAVE LEARNED FROM THE MOVIES

Should you wish to pass yourself off as a German you need not speak the language. A German accent will do.

Even when driving down a perfectly straight road it is necessary to turn the steering wheel vigorously from left to right every few moments.

The Eiffel Tower can be seen from any window in Paris.

A man will show no pain while taking the most ferocious beating but will wince in agony when a woman tries to clean his wounds.

If being chased through town, you can usually take cover in a passing St. Patrick's Day parade- at any time of the year.

AND THE MOST POPULAR ONE OF ALL....

Whenever you are in a hurry, you will never have to find your ignition keys; the car will be unlocked and started ready to go!

Annual Erection

After a few years of married life, a man finds that he is unable to perform.

He goes to his doctor, and his doctor tries a few things but nothing works.

Finally the doctor says to him: "This is all in your mind," and refers him to a psychiatrist.

After a few visits, the shrink confesses: "I am at a loss as to how you could possibly be cured." Finally the psychiatrist refers him to a witch doctor.

The witch doctor says: "I can cure this." He throws some powder on a flame, and there is a flash with billowing blue smoke. The witch doctor says:

"This is powerful healing, but you can only use it once a year! All you have to do is say '1-2-3' and it shall rise for as long as you wish!"

The guy then asks the witch doctor: "What happens when it's over?"

The witch doctor says: "All you or your partner has to say is '1234' and it will go down. But be warned; it will not work again for a year!"

The guy goes home and that night he is ready to surprise his wife with the good news So, he is lying in bed with her and says: "1-2-3" and suddenly he gets an erection.

His wife turns over and says: "What did you say '1-2-3' for?"

~~~~~~~~~~~~~~~~~~~~~~~~~

TRAVEL QUERY

One sperm says to the other, "How far is it to the ovaries?"
The other one says, "Relax. We're only just passed the tonsils."

Come Tu China

Once upon a time in China there lived two Chinamen. One named I Cum and one named No Cum. No Cum married pretty Chinese girl named No Cum Tu. For very obvious reasons, No Cum and No Cum Tu do not have any children.

One day, No Cum went out of town on business and I Cum came over and spent the night with No Cum Tu. That night I Cum came and No Cum Tu came too. This made them both very happy. However about 7 or 8 months later, No Cum saw he was about to become a father but he do not know how come, so when the baby came, he named it, How Cum U Cum. Of course, I Cum and No Cum Tu know How Cum U Cum came but to this day No Cum not know how come How Cum U Cum came!

Cum again ?

~~~~~~~~~~~~~~~~~~~~~~~

HEAVEN OR HELL?

An old lady dies and goes to heaven. She's chatting it up with St. Peter at the Pearly Gates when all of a sudden she hears the most awful, blood curdling screams.
"Don't worry about that," says St. Peter, "it's only someone having the holes put into her shoulder blades for wings."
The old lady looks a little uncomfortable but carries on with the conversation. Ten minutes later, there are more blood curdling screams. "Oh my God, "says the old lady, "now what is happening?"

"Not to worry," says St. Peter, "She's just having her head drilled to fit the halo.

"I can't do this," says the old lady, "I'm going to hell.""You can't go there," says St. Peter. "You'll be raped and sodomized."

"Maybe so," says the old lady, "but I've already got the holes drilled for that."

Breast Fed?

A woman and a baby were in the doctor's examining room, waiting for the doctor to come in for the baby's first exam. The doctor arrived, examined the baby, checked his weight, and being a little concerned, asked if thebaby was breast-fed or bottle-fed.

"Breast-fed" she replied.
"Well, strip down to your waist," the doctor ordered.
She did. He pinched her nipples, then pressed, kneaded, and rubbed both breasts for a while in a detailed examination. Motioning to her to get dressed, he said,

"No wonder this baby is underweight. You don't have any milk."

"I know," she said, "I'm his Grandma, but I'm very glad I came."

~~~~~~~~~~~~~~~~~~~~~~~~~

MAN, I FEEL LIKE A WOMAN!

A passenger plane on a cross-country trip runs into a terrible storm. The plane gets pounded by rain, hail, wind and lightening. The passengers are screaming. They are sure the plane is going to crash and they are all going to die. At the height of the storm, a young woman jumps up and exclaims, "I can't take this anymore! I can't just sit here and die like an animal, strapped into a chair.
If I am going to die, let me die feeling like a woman. Is there anyone here man enough to make me feel like a woman?"

She sees a hand raise in the back, and a handsome, tall, muscular man smiles and starts to walk up to her seat. As he approaches her, he takes off his shirt. She sees his huge muscles even in the poor lighting of the plane. He stands in front of her, shirt in hand and says to her, "I can make you feel like a woman before you die. Are you interested?"

She eagerly nods her head "yes!"

The man hands her his shirt, and he says, "Here. Iron this."

If You Read In Bed At Night.........

A typical married couple were lying in bed one night. The wife had curled up ready to go to sleep and the husband put his bed lamp on to read a book.

As he was reading, he paused and reached over to his wife and started fondling her pussy. He did this only for a very short while. Then he would stop, and resume reading his book. The wife gradually became aroused with this. Thinking that her husband was seeking some response as encouragement, before going any further, she got up and started stripping in front of him.

The husband confused, asked, "What are you doing taking all your clothes off?" The wife replied, "You were playing with my pussy, I thought it was foreplay to stimulate making love with you tonight." The husband said, "No, not at all." Then the wife asked, "Well what the hell were you doing then?"

The husband replied, "I was wetting my fingers so I could turn the pages in the book.

~~~~~~~~~~~~~~~~~~~~~~~~

MEMORY

Any married man should forget his mistakes, there's no use in two people remembering the same thing.

How Much to the Airport?

A successful businessman flew to Las Vegas for the weekend to gamble. He lost the shirt off his back, and had nothing left but a quarter and the second half of his round trip ticket. If he could just get to the airport he could get himself home. So he went out to the front of the casino where there was a cab waiting. He got in and explained his situation to the cabbie. He promised to send the driver money from home, he offered him his credit card numbers, his drivers license number, his address, etc. but to no avail. The cabbie said, "If you don't have fifteen dollars, get the hell out of my cab!" So the businessman was forced to hitch-hike to the airport and missed his flight.

One year later the businessman, having worked long and hard to regain his financial success, returned to Vegas and this time he won big.

Feeling pretty good about himself, he went out to the front of the casino to get a cab ride back to the airport. Well who should he see out there, at the end of a long line of cabs, but his old buddy who had refused to give him a ride when he was down on his luck. The businessman thought for a moment about how he could make the guy pay for his lack of charity, and he hit on a plan.

The businessman got in the first cab in the line. "How much for a ride to the airport?" he asked. "Fifteen bucks," came the reply. "And how much for you to give me a blow job on the way?" "What?! Get the hell out of my cab."

The businessman got into the back of each cab in the long line and asked the same questions, with the same result. When he got to his old friend at the back of the line, he got in and asked, "How much for a ride to the airport?" The cabbie replied, "Fifteen bucks."

The businessman said, "Ok" and off they went. Then, as they drove slowly past the long line of cabs the businessman gave a big smile and thumbs up sign to each driver.

BIG DAVE

Dave works hard at the plant and spends most evenings bowling or playing basketball at the gym.
His wife thinks he is pushing himself too hard, so for his Birthday she takes him to a local strip club.
The doorman at the club greets them and says, "Hey, Dave! How ya doin?"
His wife is puzzled and asks if he's been to this club before.
 "Oh no," says Dave. "He's on my bowling team"

When they are seated, a waitress asks Dave if he'd like his usual and brings over a Budweiser.
His wife is becoming increasingly uncomfortable and says, "How did she know that you drink Budweiser?"
 "She's in the Ladies' Bowling League, honey. We share lanes with them."

A stripper then comes over to their table, throws her arms around Dave, starts to rub herself all over him and says "Hi Davey. Want your usual table dance, big boy?"
Dave's wife, now furious, grabs her purse and storms out of the club.
Dave follows and spots her getting into a cab. Before she can slam the door, he jumps in beside her. Dave tries desperately to explain how the stripper must have mistaken him for someone else, but his wife is having none of it.
 She is screaming at him at the top of her lungs, calling him every 4 letter word in the book.
 The cabby turns his head and says, "Geez Dave, you picked up a real bitch tonight".

Brass Monkeys

During the days of wooden ships and iron men, it was necessary to keep a good supply of cannon balls near the cannon on war ships. But how to prevent them from rolling about the deck was the problem. The best storage method devised was to stack them as a square based pyramid, with one ball on top, resting on four, resting on nine, which rested on sixteen. Thus, a supply of 30 cannon balls could be stacked in a small area right next to the cannon.

There was only one problem -- how to prevent the bottom layer from sliding/rolling from under the others. The solution was a metal plate with 16 round indentations, called a Monkey. But if this plate was made of iron, the iron balls would quickly rust to it. The solution to the rusting problem was to make Brass Monkeys.
Few landlubbers realize that brass contracts much more and much faster than iron when chilled. Consequently, when the temperature dropped too far, the brass indentations would shrink so much that the iron cannon balls would come right off the monkey. Thus, it was quite literally, cold enough to freeze the balls off a brass monkey. And all this time, you thought that was a vulgar expression, didn't you?

~~~~~~~~~~~~~~~~~~~~~~~~~~

VIAGRA

A lady walked into a pharmacy and spoke to the pharmacist. She asked:
"Do you have Viagra?"
"Yes," he answered.
She asked: "Does it work?"
"Yes," he answered.
"Can you get it over the counter?" she asked.
"I can if I take two," he answered.

The Ultimate Dear John Letter

A Marine was deployed to Afghanistan.
While he was there, he received a letter from his girlfriend. In the letter she explained that she had slept with two guys while he had been gone, and that she wanted to break up with him...AND, that she wanted the pictures that he had of her back.

So, the Marine did what any squared-away Marine would do. He went around to his buddies and collected all of the unwanted photos of women that he could find.

He then mailed about 25 pictures of women (some with clothes, some without) to his girlfriend with the following note...

"I don't remember which one you are. Please remove your picture and send the rest back."

~~~~~~~~~~~~~~~~~~~~~~~~~~~~

HOW TO BATHE A CAT!

A: Put both lids of the toilet up and add the required amount of pet shampoo to the water in the bowl.
B: Pick up the cat and soothe him while you carry him towards the bathroom.
C: In one smooth movement, put the cat in the toilet and close both lids. You may need to stand on the lid.
D: The cat will self agitate and make ample suds. Never mind the noises that come from the toilet, the cat is actually enjoying this.
E: Flush the toilet three or four times. This provides a "power-wash" and "rinse."
F: Have someone open the door to the outside, be sure that there are no people between the toilet and the outside door.
G: Stand behind the toilet as far as you can, and quickly lift both lids.
H: The cat will rocket out of the toilet, and run outside where he will dry himself off.
I: Both the commode and the cat will be sparkling clean!

THE PRESIDENT'S GOLD URINAL

Before the 2001 inauguration of George Bush, he was invited to a get acquainted tour of the White House.

After drinking several glasses of iced tea, he asked Bill Clinton if he could use his personal bathroom.

When he entered Clinton's private toilet, he was astonished to see that President Clinton had a solid gold urinal.

That afternoon, George told his wife, Laura, about the urinal. "Just think," he said, "when I am president, I could have a gold urinal, too. But I wouldn't do something that self-induligible!"

Later, when Laura had lunch with Hillary at her tour of the White House, she told Hillary how impressed George had been at his discovery of the fact that, in the President's private bathroom, the President had a gold urinal.

That evening, when Bill and Hillary were getting ready for bed, Hillary smiled, and said to Bill, "I found out who pissed in your saxophone."

~~~~~~~~~~~~~~~~~~~~~~~

QUOTE OF THE YEAR

"I intend to vote Republican this year.
The Democrats left a bad taste in my mouth"

- Monica Lewinsky

AMERICA'S MOST INTELLIGENT PRESIDENT

An aircraft is about to crash.
There are five passengers on board, but unfortunately only 4 parachutes.

The first passenger says, "I'm Jonny Wilkinson, the best flyhalf in Britain. The English need me, it would be unfair to them if I died." So he takes the first parachute and jumps.

The second passenger, Graca Machel, says, "I am the wife of the former President of South Africa. I am also the most dedicated woman in the world." She takes one of the parachutes and jumps.

The third passenger, George W. Bush, says, " I am the President of the United States of America. I have a huge responsibility in world politics. And apart from that, I am the most intelligent President in the history of the country and I have a responsibility to my people not to die." So he takes a parachute and jumps.

The fourth passenger, the Pope, says to the fifth passenger, a ten year old schoolboy, "I am already old. I have already lived my life, as a good person and a priest I will give you the last parachute."

The boy replies "No problem your popeness, there is also a Parachute for you. America's most intelligent President has taken my schoolbag..."

BUSH - The Intelligence Riddle

During a recent visit to England, George W. Bush met with the Queen. He asked her, "Your Majesty, how do you run such an efficient government? Are there any tips you can give to me?" "Well," said the Queen, "the most important thing is to surround your self with intelligent people." Bush frowned. "But how do I know the people around me are really intelligent?" The Queen took a sip of tea. "Oh, that's easy. You just ask them to answer an intelligence riddle."

The Queen pushed a button on her intercom. "Please send Tony Blair in here, would you?" Tony Blair walked into the room. "Yes, Your Majesty?"

The Queen smiles. "Answer me this, please, Prime Minister. Your mother and father have a child. It is not your brother and it is not your sister. Who is it?" Without pausing for a moment, Tony Blair answered, "That would be me." "Yes! Very good," says the Queen.

Back at the White House, Bush asked to speak with vice president Dick Cheney. "Dick, answer this for me. Your mother and your father have a child. It's not your brother and it's not your sister. Who is it?"

"I'm not sure," said the Vice President. "Let me get back to you on that one."

Dick Cheney went to his advisors and asked every one, but none gave him an answer. Finally, he ended up in the men's room and recognised Colin Powell's shoes in the next stall. Dick shouted, "Colin! Can you answer this for me? Your mother and father have a child and it's not your brother or your sister. Who is it?" Colin Powell yells back, "That's easy. It's me!" Dick Cheney smiles "Thanks!"

Cheney went back to the Oval Office and to speak with Bush. "Say, I did some research and I have the answer to that riddle! It's Colin Powell."

Bush got up, stomps over to Dick Cheney, and angrily yelled into his face, "No, you blithering idiot! It's Tony Blair!"

GOOD FORTUNE?

A man is getting into the shower just as his wife is finishing up her shower when the doorbell rings. After a few seconds of arguing Over which one should go and answer the doorbell, the wife gives up, quickly wraps herself up in a towel and runs downstairs.

When she opens the door, there stands Bob, the next door Neighbour. Before she says a word, Bob says, "I'll give you £800 to drop that towel that you have on."

After thinking for a moment, the woman drops her towel and stands naked in front of Bob. After a few seconds, Bob hands her £800 and leaves.

Confused, but excited about her good fortune, the woman wraps back up in the towel and goes back upstairs.
When she gets back to the bathroom, her husband asks from the shower "Who was that?"

"It was Bob from next door," she replies. "Great," the husband says, "did he say anything about the £800 he owes me?"

~~~~~~~~~~~~~~~~~~~~~~~~~~

FDA Announcement in Pharmacology

In pharmacology, all drugs have a generic name: Tylenol is acetaminophen, Aleve is naproxen, Amoxil is amoxicillin, Advil is ibuprofen, and so on.

The FDA has been looking for a generic name for Viagra, and announced that it has settled on mycoxafloppin. Also considered were:- mycoxafailin, mydixadrupin, mydixarizin, mydixadud, dixafix, and of course, ibepokin.

WELL INFORMED

A priest was driving along and saw a nun on the side of the road, he stopped and offered her a lift which she accepted. She got in and crossed her legs, forcing her gown to open and reveal a lovely leg. The priest had a look and nearly had an accident. After controlling the car, he stealthily slid his hand up her leg.

The nun looked at him and immediately said, "Father, remember psalm 129?"

The priest was flustered and apologized profusely. He forced himself to remove his hand. However, he was unable to remove his eyes from her leg.

Further on while changing gear, he let his hand slide up her leg again. The nun once again said, "Father, remember psalm 129?"

Once again the priest apologised." Sorry sister but the flesh is weak."

Arriving at the convent, the nun got out gave him a meaningful glance and went on her way. On his arrival at the church, the priest rushed to retrieve a bible and looked up psalm 129. It Said, "Go forth and seek, further up, you will find glory."

MORAL OF THE STORY: Always be well informed in your job, or you might miss a great opportunity

~~~~~~~~~~~~~~~~~~~~~~~~~~~~

BALL SIZE

Usually the staff of the company play football.
The middle level managers are more interested in Tennis.
The top management usually has a preference for Golf.
Finding: As you go up the corporate ladder, the balls reduce in size.

LET THE BOSS GO FIRST

A sales rep, an administration clerk and the manager are walking to lunch when they find an antique oil lamp. They rub it and a Genie comes out in a puff of smoke.

The Genie says, "I usually only grant three wishes, so I'll give each of you just one."

"Me first! Me first!" says the admin clerk. "I want to be in the Bahamas, driving a speedboat, without a care in the world." Poof! She's gone.

In astonishment, "Me next! Me next!" says the sales rep. "I want to be in Hawaii, relaxing on the beach with my personal masseuse, an endless supply of pina coladas and the love of my life."
Poof! He's gone.

"OK, you're up," the Genie says to the manager.
The manager says, "I want those two back in the office after lunch."

Moral of story: always let your boss have the first say.

~~~~~~~~~~~~~~~~~~~~~~~~

Sign spotted outside a secondhand shop:

WE EXCHANGE ANYTHING - BICYCLES,
WASHING MACHINES, ETC.
WHY NOT BRING YOUR
WIFE ALONG AND GET A WONDERFUL
BARGAIN?

LAST WISH

An elderly man lay dying in his bed. In death's final agony, as he
started to slip away, he suddenly smelled the aroma of his favourite
chocolate chip cookies wafting up the stairs.

He gathered his remaining strength and lifted himself from the bed.
Leaning against the wall, he slowly made his way out of the
bedroom and, with even greater effort, he forced himself down the
stairs. Gripping the railing with both hands, he crawled downstairs
defying the pull of Morpheus.

With laboured breath, he leaned against the door-frame, gazing in
the kitchen.

Were it not for the immense pain caused by his extreme exertions
he would have thought himself already in heaven. For there spread
out upon waxed paper on the kitchen table - were hundreds of his
favourite chocolate chip cookies. Was it heaven? Or was it one final
act of heroic love from his devoted wife, seeing to it that he left this
world a happy man?

Mustering one great final effort, with tears in his eyes, he threw
himself toward the table, landing on his knees in a rumpled posture.
His parched lips parted, and the wondrous taste of the sweet
biscuit was already mentally in his mouth, seemingly bringing him
back to life.

He felt renewed strength pulsate through his body.

The aged and withered hand trembled on its way to one lone
biscuit at the edge of the table, when it was suddenly smacked with
a spatula by his wife......

"Bugger off, " she said, "they're for the funeral."

~~~~~~~~~~~~~~~~~~~~~~~~~~

SHOPPING MATHS

A man will pay £2 for a £1 item he needs.
A woman will pay £1 for a £2 item that she doesn't need.

Dictionary for Women's ads!

If you ever have trouble understanding the jargon in those PERSONAL ads........

40-ish....................	49
Adventurous..............	Slept with all your mates
Athletic.................	No tits
Average looking..........	Has a face like an arse
Beautiful................	Pathological liar
Contagious Smile.........	Does a lot of pills
Emotionally Secure.......	On medication
Feminist.................	Fat
Free spirit..............	Junkie
Fun......................	Annoying
Gentle...................	Dull
Good Listener............	Deaf
New-Age..................	Body hair problems
Open-minded..............	Desperate
Outgoing.................	Loud and Embarrassing
Poet.....................	Depressive
Professional.............	Bitch
Romantic.................	Frigid
Social...................	Fanny like a clowns pocket
Voluptuous...............	Very Fat
Large lady...............	Hugely Fat
Wants Soul mate..........	Stalker
Widow....................	Murderess

Now I understand........

Hair today............

A senior citizen's group chartered a bus from Brooklyn to Atlantic City. As they entered New Jersey, an elderly woman came up to the driver and said "I've been molested!"

The driver thought she was just being delusional, and told her to go sit back down.

10 minutes later, another old woman came forward and claimed SHE'D been molested. The driver thought he had a bus load of wackos - who'd molest them?

10 minutes later, a third came up and said she'd been molested too. The driver decided he'd had enough, and pulled into the rest stop. When he stood up, he saw an old man on his hands and knees in the aisle.

"Hey gramps, what are you doing down there?"

"I lost my toupee. Three times I thought I found it, but when I grabbed it, it ran away..."

~~~~~~~~~~~~~~~~~~~~~~~~~~~~~

HAPPINESS

To be happy with a man, you must understand him a lot and love him a little.

To be happy with a woman, you must love her a lot and not try to understand her at all.

Western or Chinese Medicine?

An American tourist goes on a trip to China. While in China, he is very sexually promiscuous and does not use a condom all the time.

A week after arriving back home in the States, he wakes one morning to find his penis covered with bright green and purple spots.

Horrified, he immediately goes to see a doctor. The doctor, never having seen anything like this before, orders some tests and tells the man to return in two days for the results. The man returns a couple of days later and the doctor says: "I've got bad news for you. You've contracted Mongolian VD. It's very rare and almost unheard of here. We know very little about it."

The man looks a little perplexed and says: "Well, give me a shot or something and fix me up, doc".

The doctor answers: "I'm sorry, there's no known cure. We're going to have to amputate your penis".

The man screams in horror, "Absolutely not! I want a second opinion". The doctor replies: "Well, it's your choice. Go ahead if you want, but surgery is your only choice".

The next day, the man seeks out a Chinese doctor, figuring that he'll know more about the disease.

The Chinese doctor examines his penis and proclaims: "Ah, yes, Mongolian VD. Vely lare disease".

The guy says to the doctor: "Yeah, yeah, I already know that, but what we can do? My American doctor wants to operate and amputate my penis?"

The Chinese doctor shakes his head and laughs: "Stupid Amelican docta, always want to opelate. Make more money, that way. No need to opelate!"

"Oh, Thank God!", the man replies.

"Yes", says the Chinese doctor,
"You no wolly! You save rots of money!"
Wait two weeks. Dick fall off by itself.

Lets Get Married!

A man met a beautiful lady and he decided he wanted to marry her right away. She said, "But we don't know anything about each other." He said, "That's all right, we'll learn about each other as we go along." So she consented, and they were married, and went on a honeymoon to a very nice resort.

One morning they were lying by the pool, when he got up off of his towel, climbed up to the 10 Meter board and did a two and a half-tuck gainer, this was followed by a three rotations in jack-knife position, where he straightened out and cut the water like a knife. After a few more demonstrations, he came back and lay down on the towel.

She said, "That was incredible!"

He said, "I used to be an Olympic diving champion. You see, I told you we'd learn more about each other as we went along."

So she got up, jumped in the pool, and started doing laps. After about thirty laps she climbed back out and lay down on her towel hardly out of breath.

He said, "That was incredible! Were you an Olympic endurance swimmer?"

"No," she said. "I was a hooker in Venice and I worked both sides of the Grand Canal."

~~~~~~~~~~~~~~~~~~~~

HUNG CHOW

Hung Chow calls his boss and says, "Hey, boss I not come work today. I really sick.

I got headache, stomach ache and my legs hurt, I not come to work". The boss says: You know Hung Chow I really need you today. When I feel like this I go to my wife and tell her to give me sex. That makes me feel better and I can go to work. You should try that.

Two hours later Hung Chow calls: "Boss, I did what you say and I feel great. I be at work soon. You got nice house" !

Little Cat Story

One day a little cat was walking through the park when he came across a pond. He peered into the pond and noticed that at the bottom of the pond there was a little cocktail sausage. The cat was feeling quite peckish so as the water wasn't that deep he reached in with his little paw and hooked the sausage out and ate it.

The next day the cat was walking through the park again and he peered into the pond again - there was another sausage but this time it was a normal sized one so The cat reached in but this time he had to put his whole front leg into the pond. The cat hooked the sausage out and ate it.

The next day the cat looked into the pond and found an enormous Cumberland sausage at the bottom of the pond - it looked so delicious but it was so deep that he had to really stretch to get it, then SPLOSH - he fell in!

The moral of this story is:

The bigger the sausage - the wetter the pussy.

~~~~~~~~~~~~~~~~~~~~~

GENERAL EQUATIONS & STATISTICS

A woman worries about the future until she gets a husband.

A man never worries about the future until he gets a wife.

A successful man is one who makes more money than his wife can spend.

A successful woman is one who can find such a man.

Hot & Cold

An elderly married couple in their 80's scheduled their annual medical examination the same day so they could travel together. After the examination, the doctor then said to the elderly man: "You appear to be in good health. Do you have any medical concerns that you would like to ask me?"

"In fact, I do," said the old man.

"After I have sex with my wife the first time, I am usually hot and sweaty, and then, after I have sex with my wife the second time, I'm usually cold and chilly."

The doctor was impressed with the octogenarian's performance yet baffled and had no answer for the old man.

After examining the elderly lady, the doctor said: "Everything appears to be fine. Do you have any medical concerns that you would like to discuss with me?"

The lady replied that she had no questions or concerns.

The doctor then asked: "Your husband had an unusual concern. He claims that he is usually hot and sweaty after having sex the first time with you and then cold and chilly after the second time. Do you know why?"

"Oh that crazy old coot!" she replied.

"That's because the first time is usually in July and the second time is usually in December!"

~~~~~~~~~~~~~~~~~~~~~

HOW TO STOP PEOPLE FROM BUGGING YOU ABOUT GETTING MARRIED:

Old aunts used to come up to me at weddings, poking me in the ribs and cackling, telling me, "You're next."

They stopped after I started doing the same thing to them at funerals.

A Christmas Story

One Christmas Eve, a frenzied young man ran into a pet shop looking for an unusual Christmas gift for his wife.

The shop owner suggested a parrot, named Chet, which could sing famous Christmas carols. This seemed like the perfect gift.

"How do I get him to sing?" The young man asked, excitedly.

"Simply hold a lighted match directly under his feet." was the shop owner's reply.

The shop owner held a lighted match under the parrot's left foot. Chet began to sing: "Jingle Bells! Jingle Bells! ..."

The shop owner then held another match under the parrot's right foot. Then Chet's tune changed, and the air was filled with: "Silent Night, Holy Night..."

The young man was so impressed that he paid the shop-keeper and ran home as quickly as he could with Chet under his arm. When the wife saw her gift she was overwhelmed.

"How beautiful!" She exclaimed, "Can he talk?"

"No," the young man replied, "But he can sing. Let me show you." So the young man whipped out his lighter and placed it under Chet's left foot, as the shop-keeper had shown him, and Chet crooned: "Jingle Bells! Jingle Bells!..." The man then moved the lighter to Chet's right foot, and out came: "Silent Night, Holy Night..."

The wife, her face filled with curiosity, then asked, "What if we hold the lighter between his legs?" The man did not know.

"Let's try it," he answered, eager to please his wife.

So they held the lighter between Chet's legs. Chet twisted his face, cleared his throat, and the little parrot sang out loudly like it was the performance of his life:

"Chet's nuts roasting on an open fire...."

MENTAL !

Jim and Mary were both patients in a Mental Hospital.

One day while they were walking past the hospital swimming pool, Mary suddenly jumped into the deep end, sunk to the bottom and stayed there.
Jim promptly jumped in to save her, he swam to the bottom and pulled Mary out - when the medical director became aware of Jim's heroic act he immediately ordered him to be discharged from the hospital, as he now considered him to be mentally stable.

When he went to tell Jim the news he said, "Jim, I have good news and bad news. The good news is you're being discharged because since you were able to jump in and save the life of another patient, I think you've regained your senses. The bad news is, Mary, the patient you saved, hung herself with her dressing gown belt in the bathroom. I am so sorry, but she's dead."
Jim replied, "She didn't hang herself. I put her there to dry."

~~~~~~~~~~~~~~~~~~~~~~~~

Fishing

One Saturday morning he gets up early, dresses quietly, gets his lunch made, puts on his long johns, grabs the dog and goes to the garage to hook up his boat to the truck and down the driveway he goes. Coming out of his garage rain is pouring down; it is like a torrential downpour. There is snow mixed in with the rain, and the wind is blowing 50 mph..
Minutes later, he returns to the garage. He comes back into the house and turns the TV to the weather channel. He finds it's going to be bad weather all day long, so he puts his boat back in the garage, quietly undresses and slips back into bed.
There he cuddles up to his wife's back, now with a different anticipation and whispers, "The weather out there is terrible." To which she sleepily replies, "Can you believe my stupid husband is out fishing in that shit?"

Cold Hands

An Amish woman and her daughter were riding in an old buggy one cold blustery day. The daughter said to her mother, "My hands are freezing cold."
The mother replied, "Put them between your legs. Your body heat will warm them up."
The daughter did and her hands warmed up.
The next day the daughter was riding in the buggy with her boyfriend who said, "My hands are freezing cold." The girl replied, "Here, put them between my legs. The warmth of my body will warm them up."
He was surprised but did and warmed his hands.

The following day the boyfriend was again in the buggy with the daughter. He said, "My nose is cold."
The girl replied "then put it between my legs. The warmth of my body will warm it up."
He did and warmed his nose.

The now excited boyfriend thinking fast said, "Gosh my penis is frozen solid."
The following day the daughter was driving in the buggy with her mother, and she says to her mother, "Have you ever heard of a penis?"
Slightly concerned the mother said, "Why, yes. Why do you ask?"
The daughter replies, "They make one heck of a mess when they defrost, don't they?

~~~~~~~~~~~~~~~~~~~~~

Fact of Life

A woman has the last word in any argument.
Anything a man says after that is the beginning of a new argument!

Chicken Sandwiches

A little boy and a little girl attended the same school and became friends. Every day they would sit together to eat their lunch. They discovered that they both brought chicken sandwiches every day! This went on all through the fourth and fifth grades until one day he noticed that her sandwich wasn't a chicken sandwich. He said, "Hey, how come you're not eating chicken, don't you like it anymore?" She said, "I love it but I have to stop eating it." "Why?" he asked. She pointed to her lap and said "Cause I'm starting to grow little feathers down there!" "Let me see," he said. "Okay" and she pulled up her skirt. He looked and said, "That's right you are, better not eat any more chicken." He kept eating his chicken sandwiches until one day he brought peanut butter. He said to the little girl, "I have to stop eating chicken sandwiches; I'm starting to get feathers down there too!" She asked if she could look so he pulled down his pants for her. She said "Oh, my God, it's too late for you; you've already got the neck and the gizzards

~~~~~~~~~~~~~~~~~~~~~~~~~~~~~~~

COCK ROOSTER

A Priest in a small rural town was very fond of the ten chickens and one handsome cock rooster he kept in a hen house behind the rectory. One Saturday night the Priest discovered that the cock rooster was missing. At the same time the Priest heard rumors of cockfights being held in town. Shocked and dismayed, he decided to say something during Sunday Mass.

During Mass he asked the congregation, "Who among you will confess to sporting a handsome cock?" All the men stood up. "No, no." he said. "That's not what I mean. Who among you will confess to having seen a handsome cock?" All the women stood up. "Oh, no," he said. "that's not what I mean, either. Who among you will confess to having seen a cock that doesn't belong to you?" Half the women stood up.

"Oh Lord," he said. "Perhaps I should rephrase the question. Has anybody seen my cock?" All the choir boys stood up.
Amen

This is the Captain Speaking...

A plane was taking off from Kennedy Airport. After reaching a comfortable cruising altitude, the captain made an announcement over the intercom, "Ladies and gentlemen, this is your captain speaking. Welcome to Flight Number 293, non-stop from New York to Los Angeles. The weather ahead is good and, therefore, we should have a smooth and uneventful flight.
Now sit back and relax.
OH, MY GOD!"

Silence followed, and after a few minutes, the captain came back on the intercom and said, "Ladies and Gentlemen, I am so sorry if I scared you earlier. While I was talking to you, the flight attendant brought me a cup of very hot coffee, which ended up spilling in my lap. You should see the front of my pants!
A passenger in Economy yelled back,
"That's nothing. You should see the back of mine!

~~~~~~~~~~~~~~~~~~~~~~~~~

Man with a strawberry stuck up his bum
goes to the doctor.
Doctor takes a look and says
"I'd better give you some cream to put on that."

GENEROUS LAWYER

One afternoon a wealthy lawyer was riding in his limousine when he saw two men along the roadside eating grass. Disturbed, he ordered his driver to stop and he got out to investigate.
He asked one man, "Why are you eating grass?"
"We don't have any money for food," the poor man replied. "We have to eat grass."
"Well, then, you can come with me to my house and I'll feed you" the lawyer said.
"But sir. I have a wife and two children with me. They are over there, under that tree"
"Bring them along," the lawyer replied. Turning to the other poor man he stated, "You come with us also."

The second man, in a pitiful voice then said, "But sir, I also have a wife and SIX children with me!"
"Bring them all, as well," the lawyer answered.

They all entered the car, which was no easy! task, even for a car as large as the limousine was.

Once underway, one of the poor fellows turned to the lawyer and said, "Sir, you are too kind. Thank you for taking all of us with you."

The lawyer replied, "Glad to do it. You'll really love my place; the grass is almost a foot high!"

~~~~~~~~~~~~~~~~~~~~~~~~

A sandwich walks into a bar.
The barman says
"Sorry, we don't serve food in here!"

EROTIC UNDIES

An Englishman, Irishman and Scotsman are all watching their wive's play in a Ladies match at the local club.

The Englishman's wife steps up to the tee and as she bends over to place her ball, a gust of wind blows up her skirt revealing a lack of underwear.

"GOOD GOD! Why aren't you wearing any knickers?" her husband demanded.
"Well, you don't give me enough housekeeping money to afford to buy any."
The Englishman immediately reaches into his pocket and says, "For the sake of decency here's fifty pounds, now go buy yourself some underwear."

Next the Irishman's wife bends over to tee up her ball. Her skirt blows up, revealing she too is wearing no undies.
"Bejesus woman. You've no knickers-why not?" She replies, "I cannot afford 'em on the money you give me."
He reaches into his pocket and says "For the sake of decency here's twenty pounds, go buy yourself some underwear!"

Lastly, the Scotsman wife bends over. The wind also takes her skirt clear over her head to reveal that she is naked under it.
"Hoot, lassie! Why d'ye have no knickers?"
She too explains, "You don't give me enough housekeeping money to be able to afford any."

The Scot reaches into his pocket and says, "For the sake of decency here's my comb. Tidy yourself up a bit."

~~~~~~~~~~~~~~~~~~~~~~~~

Two aerials meet on a roof, fall in love get married.
The ceremony was rubbish but the reception
was brilliant.

Where's the John?

An American tourist in London decides to skip his tour group and explore the city on his own.
He wanders around, seeing the sights, and occasionally stopping at a quaint pub to soak up the local culture, chat with the lads, and have a pint of Guinness.

After a while, he finds himself in a very high class neighborhood.... big, stately residences ... no pubs, no stores, no restaurants, and worst of all.... NO PUBLIC RESTROOMS.

He really, has to go, after all that Guinness. He finds a narrow side street, with high walls surrounding the adjacent buildings and decides to use the wall to solve his problem.

As he is unzipping, he is tapped on the shoulder by a London Bobbie, who says, "I say, sir, you simply cannot do that here, you know."
"I'm very sorry, officer," replies the American, "but I really, really HAVE TO GO, and I just can't find a public restroom."

"Ah, yes," said the Bobbie..."Just follow me." He leads him to a back "delivery alley," then along a wall to a gate, which he opens.
"In there," points the Bobbie. "Whiz away, ... anywhere you want."

The fellow enters and finds himself in the most beautiful garden he has ever seen. Manicured grass lawns, statuary, fountains, sculptured hedges, and huge beds of gorgeous flowers, all in perfect bloom. Since he has the cop's blessing, he zips down and unburdens himself and is greatly relieved.

As he goes back through the gate, he says to the Bobbie "That was really decent of you .. is that "British Hospitality ?"

"No" replied the Bobbie, with a satisfied smile on his face, "that is the French Embassy."

Woodcutter

One day, while a woodcutter was cutting a branch of a tree above a river, his axe fell into the river.

When he cried out, the Lord appeared and asked, "Why are you crying?"

The woodcutter replied that his axe has fallen into water.

The Lord went down into the water and reappeared with a golden axe.

"Is this your axe?" the Lord asked. The woodcutter replied, "No."

The Lord again went down and came up with a silver axe. "Is this your axe?" the Lord asked.

Again, the woodcutter replied, "No." The Lord went down again and came up with an iron axe. "Is this your axe?" the Lord asked. The woodcutter replied, "Yes."

The Lord was pleased with the man's honesty and gave him all three axes to keep, and the woodcutter went home happily.

One day while he was walking with his wife along the riverbank, the woodcutter's wife fell into the river. When he cried out, the Lord again appeared and asked him, "Why are you crying?"

"Oh Lord, my wife has fallen into the water!"

The Lord went down into the water and came up with Jennifer Lopez. "Is this your wife?" the Lord asked. "Yes," cried the woodcutter.

The Lord was furious. "You cheat! That is an untruth!" The woodcutter replied, "Oh, forgive me, my Lord. It is a misunderstanding.

You see, if I said 'no' to Jennifer Lopez, You will come up with Catherine Zeta-Jones. Then if I also say 'no' to her, You will thirdly come up with my wife, and I will say 'yes,' and then all three will be given to me.

But Lord, I am a poor man and I will not be able to take care of all three wives, so that's why I said yes this time."

The moral of the story is whenever a man lies it is for an honourable and useful reason

PROSTITUTES APPEAL TO THE POPE

~~~~~~~~~~~~~~~~~~~~~~~~~

SHOT OFF WOMAN'S LEG HELPS NICKLAUS TO 66

HAPPY GARDENING!!!

The teenage grand daughter comes downstairs for her date with a see thru blouse on and no bra.
Her grandmother pitches a fit, telling her not to dare go out like that.

The teenager tells her "loosen up Grams, these are modern times and you have to let your rosebuds show", and out she goes.

The next day the teenager comes downstairs and the grandmother is sitting there with no top on. The teenager wants to die. She explains to the grandmother that she has friends coming over and it is not appropriate to be dressed that way.

The grandmother says, "Loosen up sweetie, if you can show off your rosebuds then I can display my hanging baskets."

Happy Gardening!

~~~~~~~~~~~~~~~~~~~~~~~~

USED CONDOMS

What do you do with 365 used condoms?

Melt them down, make a tyre and call it a Good Year!

Check your Underwear Martin!!

Martin went to the doctor suffering from severe headaches. After a thorough examination, the doctor turned to him and said: "Martin, the good news is I can cure your headaches.
The bad news is that it will require castration." "You have a very rare condition, which causes your testicles to press on your spine, and the pressure creates these serious headaches you've been experiencing.
So the only way to relieve the pressure is to remove the testicles."

Martin was shocked and depressed. He wondered if he had anything to live for. He couldn't concentrate long enough to answer, but decided he had no choice but to go under the knife.

When he eventually left the hospital Martin was pleasantly surprised at how good it felt not to have a headache for the first time in 20 years, but he also knew that he was missing an important part of himself.

As he walked down the street, he realized that he felt like a different person. He could make a fresh start and live a new life. He saw a men's clothing store and thought to himself a new suit would be the perfect thing to mark this new beginning. He entered the shop and told the salesman: "I'd like a new suit."
The elderly tailor eyed him briefly and said: "Let's see... size 44 long?"
"That's right, how did you know?" said Martin, laughing.
"I've been in the business 60 years!" replied the tailor.
Martin tried on the suit and it fitted like a glove. As Martin admired himself in the mirror, the salesman asked:
"How about a new shirt?" Martin thought for a moment and then agreed. The salesman eyed Martin again.
"Let's see... 34 sleeve and 16-and-a-half neck?" Once again, Martin was surprised.
"That's right, how did you know?"
"Like I said, I've been in the business 60 years!"
So Martin tried on the shirt, and it was a perfect fit. As Martin adjusted the collar in the mirror, the salesman asked:
"How about new shoes?" Martin was on a roll and so thought, why

not? So the salesman eyed Martin's feet and said:

"Let's see... you must be a size nine-and-a-half?"

Martin was astonished. "That's right, how did you know?"

"Well, young fella, I've been in the business long enough to know these things!" Martin tried on the shoes and they were also a remarkable fit. Martin walked comfortably around the shop and the salesman asked:

"So that only leaves the new underwear. How about it?" Martin thought for a second and agreed. The salesman stepped back, eyed Martin's waist and said:

"Let's see... size 36.

Martin laughed. "Ah ha! I got you! I've worn size 34 since I was 18 years old "

The salesman shook his head.

"There's no way. I'm never wrong. You can't wear a size 34."

"Oh yes I can," replied Martin and have been most of my life.

"I don't understand," said the tailor.

"By my reckoning a 34 underwear would press your testicles up against the base of your spine and give you one hell of a headache."

Donkey Raffle

Smitty left Newfoundland and moved to Toronto and bought a
donkey from an old farmer for $100. The farmer agreed to deliver
the donkey the next day. The following day, the farmer drove up and
said, "I'm sorry, but I have some bad news... the donkey died last
night."
"Well, den" said Smitty,
"Just give my money back den."
"I can't do that, sir. I spent it already."
"OK, den. Just unload dat donkey." "What are you gonna do with
him?"
"I'm gonna raffle him off."
"You can't raffle a dead donkey, you dumb Newfie!"
"Well dat's where you're wrong. You wait you an' you'll learn how
smart we Newfies are!

A month later, the farmer ran into the Newfie and asked, "What
happened with that dead donkey?"
"I raffled dat donkey off. I sold 500 tickets at two dollars each and
made $998." "Didn't anyone complain?"
"Just dat guy who won. So I gave him his two dollars back."

~~~~~~~~~~~~~~~~~~~~~~~~~~~

Things I've Learned from My Children

A king size waterbed holds enough water to fill a 3 bedroom house
4 inches deep.

~~~~~~~~~~

A 3-year olds voice is louder than 200 adults in a crowded
restaurant.

~~~~~~~~~~

You should not throw balls up when the ceiling fan is on, using the
ceiling fan as a bat; you have to throw the ball up a few times before
you get a hit. A ceiling fan can then hit a ball a long way.
The glass in windows (even double-glazing) doesn't stop a ball hit by
a ceiling fan.

Speaking English Could Kill You!

The Japanese eat very little fat and suffer fewer heart attacks than the British or Americans.
The French eat a lot of fat and also suffer fewer heart attacks than the British or Americans.

The Japanese drink very little red wine and suffer fewer heart attacks than the British or Americans.
The Italians drink excessive amounts of red wine and also suffer fewer heart attacks than the British or Americans.

CONCLUSION:
Eat and drink what you like.
Speaking English is apparently what kills you.

~~~~~~~~~~~~~~~~~~~~~~~~~

LEAKY BATH?

Paddy walks into a hardware shop, buys a bath, and has it delivered to his home.
Next day he walks back into the shop and says ' that bath you sold me leaks.'
'Paddy' says the shopkeeper ' did you buy a plug ?'
'Jasus' says Paddy. 'You never told me it was electric.'

Three Bears

Frank was excited about his new rifle and decided to try bear hunting.
He travels to Alaska and spots a small brown bear and shoots it.

Right after, there was a tap on his shoulder and he turned to see a big black bear. The big black bear said, "That was a very bad mistake ... that was my cousin and I'm going to give you two choices... Either I maul you to death or we have sex."

After considering briefly, Frank decided to accede the latter alternative.

So the black bear had his way with Frank. Even though he felt sore for two weeks, Frank soon recovered and vowed revenge.

He headed out on another trip to Alaska where he found the black bear and shot it dead. Right after, there was another tap on his shoulder. This time a huge grizzly bear stood right next to him.
The grizzly said "That was a big mistake, Frank. That was my cousin and you've got two choices. Either I maul you to death or we have rough sex".
Again Frank thought it better to cooperate with the grizzly bear than be mauled to death. So the grizzly has his way with Frank. Although he survived, it took several months before Frank finally recovered.

Now, Frank is completely outraged, he headed back to Alaska and managed to track down that grizzly bear and shot it.
He felt sweet revenge, but then, he felt a tap on his shoulder. He turned to see a giant polar bear standing there.

The polar bear looked at him very sadly and said,

"Admit it Frank, you don't come here for the hunting, do you?"

Sad News

It is with the saddest heart that I must pass on the following news: Please join me in remembering a great icon of the entertainment community.

The Pillsbury Doughboy died yesterday of a yeast infection, and complications from repeated pokes in the belly.

He was 71.
Doughboy was buried in a lightly greased coffin. Dozens of celebrities turned out to pay their respects, including Mrs. Butterworth, Hungry Jack, the California Raisins, Betty Crocker, the Hostess Twinkies, and Captain Crunch.

His grave site was piled high with flours.
Aunt Jemima delivered the Eulogy and lovingly described Doughboy as a man who never knew how much he was kneaded.

Doughboy rose quickly in the show business, but his life was filled with turnovers.

He was not considered a very smart cookie, wasting much of his dough on half-baked schemes. Despite being a little flaky at times, he still, as a crusty old man, was considered a roll model for millions.

Doughboy is survived by his wife, Play Dough; two children, John Dough and Jane Dough; plus they had one in the oven.
He is also survived by his elderly father, Pop Tart.

The funeral was held at 350 for about 20 minutes.

Clever Diagnosis

A young doctor had moved out to a small community to replace a doctor who was retiring. The older doctor suggested the young one accompany him on his rounds so the community could become used to a new doctor.

At the first house a woman complained, "I've been a little sick to my stomach." The older doctor said, "Well, you've probably been overdoing the fresh fruit. Why not cut back on the amount you've been eating and see if that does the trick?"

As they left the younger man said, "You didn't even examine that woman. How'd you come to your diagnosis so quickly?" "I didn't have to. You noticed I dropped my stethoscope on the floor in there? When I bent over to pick it up I noticed a half dozen banana peels in the trash. That was what was probably making her sick."

"Huh," the younger doctor said, "Pretty clever. I think I'll try that at the next house." Arriving at the next house, they spent several minutes talking with a younger woman. She complained that she just didn't have the energy she once did. "I'm feeling terribly run down lately."
"You've probably been doing too much work for the church," the younger doctor told her. "Perhaps you should cut back a bit and see if that helps."
As they left, the elder doc said, Your diagnosis is almost certainly correct but how did you arrive at it?
"Well, just like you did at the last house, I dropped my stethoscope and when I bent down to retrieve it, I noticed the preacher under the bed."

ALL THE DRINKS ON THE HOUSE

An Irishman, an Englishman, and a Scot were sitting in a bar. The view was fantastic, the beer excellent, and the food exceptional. "Y'know" said the Scot, "I still prefer the pubs back home. Why in Glasgow there's a little bar called McTavish's where the owner will buy your 5th drink after you buy 4."

"Well" said the Englishman, "at my local, the Red Lion, the barman there will buy your 3rd drink after you buy the first 2."

"Ahhh that's nothing" said the Irishman. "Back home in Dublin there's Ryan's bar. Now the moment you set foot in the place they'll buy you a drink, then another, all the drinks you like. Then when you've had enough they'll take you upstairs and see that you get laid. All on the house."

The Englishman and the Scot immediately pour scorn on the Irishman's claims. He swears every word is true. "Well" said the Englishman, "did this actually happen to you?"
"No, not me personally," said the Irishman. "But it did happen to my sister."

~~~~~~~~~~~~~~~~~~~~~~~

GOLF GUN

Two Mexican detectives were investigating the murder of Juan Gonzalez.
"How was he killed?" asked one detective.
"With a golf gun," the other detective replied.
"A golf gun?! What is a golf gun?"
"I don't know. But it sure made a hole in Juan."

The Poor Box

A married man goes into the confessional and says to his priest, I had an affair with a woman. . . almost. . .."

The priest asks, "What do you mean, almost?"
The man says, "Well, we got undressed and rubbed together, but then we stopped."
The priest says, "Rubbing together is the same as putting it in. You're not to see that woman again. For your penance, say 5 Hail Mary's and put £50 in the poor box."

The man leaves the confessional, says his prayers, then walks over to the poor box. He pauses for a moment with £50 in his hand, then starts to leave. The priest, who was watching, quickly runs over to him saying,

"I saw that, you didn't put any money in the poor box!"
The man replies, "Yeah, but I rubbed the £50 on the box, and apparently that's the same as putting it in."

~~~~~~~~~~~~~~~~~~~~~~~~~~

Things I've Learned from My Children

When you hear the toilet flush and the words "uh oh," it's already too late.

~~~~~~~~~~~

Superglue IS forever !

~~~~~~~~~~~

If you hook a dog leash over a ceiling fan, the motor is not strong enough to rotate a 42 pound boy wearing Batman underwear and a Superman cape.
It is strong enough, however, if tied to a paint can, to spread paint on all four walls of a large room.

Unattended Luggage!

Yesterday, I was on the Underground travelling on the Northern line. A man of Arabic-appearance got off the train and I noticed that he had left his bag behind. I grabbed the bag and ran after him, caught up with him at the top of the escalator and handed him back his bag.

He was extremely grateful to me and reached into his bag which appeared to contain large bundles of banknotes and white powder. He looked round, Made sure nobody was looking and whispered to me:

"I can never repay your kindness sir, but I will try to with a word of advice for you: Stay away from Slough."

I was terrified. "Is there going to be an attack?" I whispered.

"No, sir" he whispered back "It's a shit hole."

~~~~~~~~~~~~~~~~~~~~~~~~~~~~

OPERATION NERVES?

Two little boys are in a hospital, lying on stretchers next to each other, outside the operating room. The first kid leans over and asks, "What are you in here for? "
The second kid says, "I'm in here to get my tonsils out and I'm a little nervous. The first kid says, "You've got nothing to worry about. I had that done when I was four.
They put you to sleep, and when you wake up they give you lots of Jelly and ice cream. It's a breeze."

The second kid then asks, "What are you here for?" The first kid says,
"A Circumcision." And the second kid says,
"Whoa, Good luck buddy, I had that done when I was born. Couldn't walk for a year."

BAAAAAAH !

A Welsh man buys several sheep, hoping to breed them for wool. After several weeks, he notices that none of the sheep are getting pregnant, and phones a vet for help. The vet tells him that he should try artificial insemination.

The farmer doesn't have the slightest idea what this means but, not wanting to display his ignorance, only asks the vet how he will know when the sheep are pregnant.
The vet tells him that they will stop standing around and instead will lie down and wallow in grass when they are pregnant.

The man hangs up and gives it some thought. He comes to the conclusion that artificial insemination means he has to impregnate the sheep himself. So, he loads the sheep into his Land Rover, drives them out into the woods, has sex with them all, brings them back, and goes to bed.

Next morning, he wakes and looks out at the sheep. Seeing that they are all still standing around, he deduces that the first try didn't take, and loads them in the Land Rover again.
He drives them out to the woods, bangs each sheep twice for good measure, brings them back, and goes to bed exhausted.

In the morning, he wakes to find the sheep still just standing round. Try again. he tells himself, and proceeds to load them up, and drive them out to the woods. He spends all day shagging the sheep and upon returning home, falls listlessly into bed.

The 4th morning, he cannot even raise himself from the bed to look out of the window. He asks his wife to look, and tell him if the sheep are lying in the grass.

No, she says, they're all in the Land Rover, and one of them is beeping the horn.

JUVENILE COURT TO TRY SHOOTING DEFENDANTS

~~~~~~~~~~~~~~~~~~~~~~~~~~~~~~

TWO SOVIET SHIPS COLLIDE, ONE DIES

Why We Love Children....

A nursery school pupil told his teacher he'd found a cat, but it was dead.
"How do you know that the cat was dead?" she asked her pupil.
"Because I pissed in its ear and it didn't move," answered the child innocently.
"You did what?" said the teacher
"You know," explained the boy,
"I leaned over and went 'Pssst!' and it didn't move."

~~~~~~~~~~~~~~~~~~~~~~~~~~~~~~~~

One day the first grade teacher was reading the story of Chicken Little to her class. She came to the part of the story where Chicken Little tried to warn the farmer.
She read, "....
and so Chicken Little went up to the farmer and said, "The sky is falling, the sky is falling!"
The teacher paused then asked the class, "And what do you think that farmer said?"
One little girl raised her hand and said,
"He probably said: 'Holy Shit! A talking chicken!'"
The teacher was unable to teach for the next 10 minutes.

~~~~~~~~~~~~~~~~~~~~~~~~~~~~~~~~

A ten year old girl goes to the barber shop with her father. She stands right next to the barber chair, eating a Snickers bar while her dad gets his hair cut.
The barber says to her, "Sweetheart, don't stand too close, you're gonna get hair in your Snickers"

She says, "Yeah, I know, and I'm gonna grow BOOBS too!"

ROYS NEW BOOTS

Roy always wanted a pair of authentic cowboy boots. Seeing some on sale one day, he buys them, wears them home, walking proudly. He walks into the house and says to his wife: "Notice anything different about me?"

Bessie looks him over "Nope."

Frustrated, Roy storms off into the bathroom, undresses, and walks back into the room completely naked, except for the boots. Again, he asks, a little louder this time,
"Notice anything DIFFERENT NOW?"

Bessie looks up and says, "Roy, what's different? It's hanging down today, it was hanging down yesterday, it'll be hanging down again tomorrow.

Furious, Roy yells,
"AND DO YOU KNOW WHY IT IS HANGING DOWN, BESSIE? IT'S HANGING DOWN BECAUSE IT'S LOOKING AT MY NEW BOOTS!!!!!"

To which Bessie replies, "Should have bought a hat, Roy!"

~~~~~~~~~~~~~~~~~~~~~~~~~~~

Sean Connery gets a call from his agent one day.
The agent says
"Sean, I've got you a job, starts tomorrow, early. You'll have to be there for 10-ish".
Sean furrows his brow and says , "Tennish? but I don't even have a racket

THE WORST SCHOOL REPORT

A mother enters her daughter's bedroom and sees a letter on the bed. With much foreboding and trembling hands she opens and reads it:

Dear Mum

It is with great regret and sorrow that I must tell you I have decided to elope with my new boyfriend. He is so nice with all his body piercing, tattoos and big motorbike. I've found real love and passion Mum. I'm pregnant too and Ahmed says we will be very comfortable in his old caravan in the woods. He wants to have many more children with me and that's one of my dreams. I've learned that marijuana doesn't hurt anyone, so we'll be growing it for us and his friends who are providing all the cocaine and ecstasy we need. In the meantime, we pray that science finds a cure for AIDS so Ahmed can get better, he deserves it.
Don't worry Mum, I'm 15 years old now and I know how to take care of myself. Some day I'll visit so you can get to know your grandchildren.

Your loving daughter,

Judith

PS: Only kidding Mum, I'm over at Julie's house. I just wanted to show you there are worse things in life than my school report, which you'll find under the pillow.

Royal Wedding

Every royal wedding reminds me of a story that was current after Charles and Di were married:

On the day of the wedding, Di was getting dressed, surrounded by all her family, and she suddenly realised she had forgotten to get any shoes.
Panic. Then her sister remembered that she had a pair of white shoes from her wedding so she lent them to Di for the day. Unfortunately they were a bit too small and by the time the festivities were over Di's feet were agony. When she and Charlie withdrew to their room the only thing she could think of was getting her shoes off.

The rest of the Royal Family crowded round the door to the bedroom and they heard roughly what they expected: grunts, straining noises and the occasional muffled scream. Eventually they heard Charlie say 'God, that was tight.
'There,' whispered the Queen. 'I told you she was a virgin.'
Then, to their surprise, they heard Charlie say.
'Right. Now for the other one.' Followed by more grunting and straining and at last Charlie said.
'My God. That was even tighter.'

'That's my boy,' said the Duke. 'Once a sailor, always a sailor.'

~~~~~~~~~~~~~~~~~~~~~~~~

Scientists today exhumed Beethoven from his grave; when they opened the coffin, they were shocked to see him playing the piano backwards.
When asked what this meant a spokesman said he was de-composing.

Ground Control to Major Tom

Here are some conversations that passengers normally don't hear. The following are accounts of actual exchanges between airline pilots and control towers from around the world:

The German air controllers at Frankfurt Airport are a short-tempered lot. They not only expect one to know one's gate parking location, but how to get there without any assistance from them. So it was with some amusement that we (a Pan Am 747) listened to the following exchange between Frankfurt ground control and a British Airways 747, call sign "Speedbird 206": Speedbird 206: "Frankfurt, Speedbird 206 clear of active runway."
Ground: "Speedbird 206. Taxi to gate Alpha One-Seven." The BA 747 pulled onto the main taxiway and slowed to a stop. Ground: "Speedbird, do you not know where you are going?" Speedbird 206: "Stand by, Ground, I'm looking up our gate location now." Ground (with arrogant impatience): "Speedbird 206, haff you not been to Frankfurt before?" Speedbird 206 (coolly): "Yes, twice in 1944 but I didn't stop."

O'Hare Approach Control: "United 329 heavy, your traffic is a Fokker, one o'clock, three miles, eastbound."
United 329: "Approach, I've always wanted to say this... I've got the little Fokker in sight."

A Pan Am 727 flight engineer waiting for start clearance in Munich overheard the following: Lufthansa (in German): "Ground, what is our start clearance time?" Ground (in English): "If you want an answer you must speak English." Lufthansa (in English): "I am a German, flying a German airplane, in Germany. Why must I speak English?" Unknown voice (in a beautiful British accent): "Because you lost the bloody war!"

COUGH SYRUP

John was a clerk in a small drugstore but he was not much of
a salesman. He could never find the item the customer wanted.
Bob, the owner, had had about enough and warned John that the
next sale he missed would be his last.

Just then a man came in coughing and he ask John for their
best cough syrup. Try as he might John could not find the
cough syrup. Remembering Bob's warning he sold the man a box
of Ex-Lax and told him to take it all at once. The customer
did as John said and then walked outside and leaned against
a lamp post.

Bob had seen the whole thing and came over to ask John what
had transpired.

"He wanted something for his cough but I couldn't find the
cough syrup. I substituted Ex-Lax and told him to take it
all at once," John explained.

"Ex-Lax won't cure a cough" Bob shouted angrily.

"Sure it will" John said, pointing at the man leaning on
the lamp post. "Look at him. He's afraid to cough!"

~~~~~~~~~~~~~~~~~~~~~~~~~~

FLASHER

Three old ladies named Gertrude, Maude, and Tilly were sitting on a
park bench having a quiet conversation.
Suddenly a flasher approached from across the park. The flasher
came up to the ladies, stood right in front of them and opened his
trench coat.

Gertrude immediately had a stroke.
Then Maude also had a stroke.
But Tilly, being older and more feeble, couldn't reach that far

BULLS TESTICLES

An American touring Spain stopped at a local restaurant following a day of sightseeing.

While sipping his sangria, he noticed a sizzling, scrumptious looking platter being served at the next table. Not only did it look good, the smell was wonderful. He asked the waiter, "What is that you just served?" The waiter replied, " Ah senor, you have excellent taste! Those are bulls testicles from the bull fight this morning. A delicacy!" The American, though momentarily daunted, said, "What the hell, I'm on vacation! Bring me an order!" The waiter replied, "I am so sorry senor. There is only one serving per day because there is only one bull fight each morning. If you come early tomorrow and place your order, we will be sure to save you this delicacy!"

The next morning, the American returned, placed his order, and then that evening he was served the one and only special delicacy of the day.

After a few bites, and inspecting the contents of his platter, he called to the waiter and said, "These are delicious, but they are much, much smaller than the ones I saw you serve yesterday!"

The waiter shrugged his shoulders and replied,
"Si senor. Sometimes the bull wins."

~~~~~~~~~~~~~~~~~~~~~~~~

Things I've Learned from My Children

Always look in the oven before you turn it on. Plastic toys do not like ovens.

~~~~~~~~~~~

The average response time for the fire brigade is about 20 minutes.

~~~~~~~~~

The spin cycle on the washing machine does not make earthworms dizzy. It will, however, make cats dizzy.
Cats throw up twice their body weight when dizzy.

THE LAST CONFESSION
OF A DYING MAN

Jake was dying. His wife, Becky, was maintaining a candlelight vigil by his side. She held his fragile hand, tears running down her face. Her praying roused him from his slumber. He looked up and his pale lips Began to move slightly.
"Becky my darling," he whispered.
"Hush my love," she said. "Rest, don't talk."
He was insistent. "Becky," he said in his tired voice, "I have something that I must confess."
"There's nothing to confess," replied the weeping Becky, "everything's all right, go to sleep."
"No, no. I must die in peace, Becky. I slept with your sister, your best friend, and her best friend!"
"I know, my sweet one," whispered Becky, "now go to sleep and let the poison work."

~~~~~~~~~~~~~~~~~~~~~~~~

OOH - ERR!

A passenger in a taxi tapped the driver on the shoulder to ask him something. The driver screamed, lost control of the cab, nearly hit a bus, drove up over the curb, and stopped just inches from a large plate glass window. For a few moments everything was silent in the cab, then the driver said, "Please, don't ever do that again. You scared the daylights out of me."
The passenger, who was also frightened, apologised and said he didn't realise that a tap on the shoulder could frighten him so much, to which the driver replied:
"I'm sorry, it's really not your fault at all. Today is my first day driving a cab. I have been driving a hearse for the last 25 years!

Lay-Off

It was the end of the financial year and Dave had been told by his boss that to achieve end of year figures, he would have to let someone in the office go. This put Dave in a very awkward position, as he was more than happy with everybody's performance over the last 12 months. He decided to sleep on it that night, in order to make the best decision for the company.

All the way to work the next day, he was still undecided between two of his staff, Dawn & Jack, which one was to be the unlucky person. After much deliberation, he decided that whoever was first to the water fountain for a drink would be the one for the chop. Everyone arrived at 9:00am as usual & Dave sat in his office waiting for Dawn or Jack to make the move.
At 9:30 Dawn got up & went straight to the fountain. As soon as she turned towards Dave's office he called her over. "Please sit down Dawn" said Dave, "I am afraid I have to either lay you or Jack off". Dawn turned to him & replied......

"I was out 'til late last night & still have a bit of a hangover, so do me a favour & Jack off!!!!"

~~~~~~~~~~~~~~~~~~~~~~~~~~~~

I Don't Like the Look of Your Wife

A doctor examined a woman, took the husband aside, and said, "I don't like the looks of your wife at all".
"Me neither doc," said the husband. "But she's a great cook and really good with the kids."

The Best Toast

John O'Reilly hoisted his beer at the pub and said," Here's to spending the rest of me life, between the legs of me wife!"

That won him the top prize for the best toast of the night. He went home and told his wife, Mary, "I won the prize for the best toast of the night."
She said, "Aye, what was your toast?"
John said, "Here's to spending the rest of me life, sitting in church beside me wife."
"Oh, that is very nice indeed, John!" Mary said.

The next day, Mary ran into one of John's toasting buddies on the street corner. The man chuckled leeringly and said, "John won the prize the last night with a toast about you, Mary."
She said, "Aye, and I was a bit surprised meself! You know, he's only been there twice. Once he fell asleep, and the other time I had to pull him by the ears to make him come."

~~~~~~~~~~~~~~~~~~~~~~~~~~

A VISION

A man left work one Friday afternoon. But instead of going home, he stayed out the entire weekend, hunting with the boys & spending his entire weeks wages.
When he finally appeared at home, Sunday night, he was confronted by his very angry wife and was barraged for nearly 2 hours with a tirade about his actions.
Finally his wife stopped the nagging and simply said to him "How would you like it if you didn't see me for 2 or 3 days?"
To which he replied, "That would be fine with me."
Monday went by & he didn't see his wife. Tuesday & Wednesday came & went and he didn't see her.
On Thursday, the swelling went down just enough where he could see her a little out of the corner of his left eye.

Don't Step on the Ducks!

Three women die together in an accident and go to heaven. When they get there, St. Peter says, "We only have one rule here in heaven ...don't step on the ducks."

So they enter heaven, and sure enough, there are ducks all over the place. It is almost impossible not to step on a duck, and although they try their best to avoid them, the first woman accidentally steps on one. Along comes St. Peter with the ugliest man she ever seen. St. Peter chains them together and says, "Your punishment for stepping on a duck is to spend eternity chained to this ugly man!"

The next day, the second woman accidentally steps on a duck, and along comes St. Peter, who doesn't miss a thing, and with him is another extremely ugly man. He chains them together with the same punishment as the first woman.

The third woman has observed all this and, not wanting to be chained for all eternity to an ugly man, is very, VERY careful where she steps. She manages to go months without stepping on any ducks, until one day St. Peter comes up to her with the most handsome man she has ever laid eyes on. St. Peter chains them together without saying a word.

The woman remarks, "I wonder what I did to deserve being chained to you for all of eternity?"

And the guy says, "Well, I don't know what you did, but I stepped on a duck."

~~~~~~~~~~~~~~~~~~~~~~~~~~~~

Sex Before Marriage

Two guys were discussing popular family trends on sex, marriage, and values.

Stu said, "I didn't sleep with my wife before we got married, did you?"

Leroy replied, "I'm not sure, what was her maiden name?"

MONKS

A new young monk arrives at the monastery. He is assigned to help the other monks in copying the old canons and laws of the church by hand.

He notices - however - that all of the monks are copying from copies - not from the original manuscript.

So - the new monk goes to the abbot to question this - pointing out that if someone made even a small error in the first copy - it would never be picked up. In fact - that error would be continued in all of the subsequent copies.

The Abbot says, "We have been copying from the copies for centuries - but you make a good point, my son".

So - he goes down into the dark caves underneath the monastery where the original manuscript is held in a locked vault that hasn't been opened for hundreds of years.

Several days go by and nobody sees the old abbot. So - the young monk gets worried and goes downstairs to look for him. He sees him banging his head against the wall. His forehead is all bloody and bruised and he is crying uncontrollably.

The young monk asks the old abbot, "What's wrong father?"

In a choking voice - the old abbot replies -

"You were right son, I've checked through and found one single mistake in the original canons"

"Yes ok, but why are you banging your head against the wall so hard?" said the young monk

"The misspelled word is celebrate."

~~~~~~~~~~~~~~~~~~~~~~~~~

Intelligence?

A little boy went up to his father and asked: "Dad, where did all of my intelligence come from?"

The father replied. "Well son, you must have got it from your mother, cause I still have mine"

Was Jesus BLACK, JEWISH, ITALIAN, CALIFORNIAN, IRISH or simply a Woman?

There were 3 good arguments that Jesus was Black:
1. He called everyone "brother".
2. He liked Gospel.
3. He couldn't get a fair trial.

But then there were 3 equally good arguments that Jesus was Jewish:
1. He went into His Father's business.
2. He lived at home until he was 33.
3. He was sure his Mother was a virgin and his mother was sure He was God.

But then there were 3 equally good arguments that He was Italian:
1. He talked with his hands.
2. He had wine with every meal.
3. He used olive oil.

But then there were 3 equally good arguments that He was a Californian:
1. He never cut his hair.
2. He walked around barefoot all the time.
3. He started a new religion.

But then there were 3 equally good arguments that He was Irish:
1. He never got married.
2. He was always telling stories.
3. He loved green pastures.

But the most compelling evidence of all---3 proofs that Jesus was a woman:
1. He fed a crowd at a moment's notice when there was no food.
2. He kept trying to get a message across to a bunch of men who just didn't get it.
3. And even when he was dead, He had to get up because there was more work to do.

A Female Brain is So Cheap!

In the hospital, the relatives gathered in the waiting room, where their family member lay gravely ill. Finally, the doctor came in, looking tired and somber. "I'm afraid I'm the bearer of bad news," he said as he surveyed the worried faces. "The only hope left for your loved one at this time is a brain transplant. It's an experimental procedure, semi-risky -- and you will have to pay for the brain yourselves." The family members sat silent as they absorbed the news.
After a great length of time, someone asked,"Well,how much does a brain cost?" The doctor quickly responded, "£5,000 for a male brain, and £200 for a female brain.
" The moment turned awkward. Men in the room tried not to smile, avoiding eye contact with the women, but some actually smirked. Finally, one man, unable to control his curiosity, blurted out the question everyone wanted to ask: "Why does the male brain cost so much more?" The doctor smiled at his childish innocence, and so, to the entire group he said, "It's just standard pricing procedure. We have to mark down the price of the female brains, because they've actually been used."

~~~~~~~~~~~~~~~~~~~~~~~~~~~~~

OOOOPS!

The state of Michigan has been laughing for days, and a very embarrassed female news anchor will probably from now on think before she speaks.

What happens when you predict snow but don't get any.
The female news anchor who, the day after it was supposed to have snowed and didn't, turned to the weatherman and asked
"So Bob, where's that 8 inches you promised me last night?"

He was laughing so hard he had to leave the set.

The Elmo Factory

There is a factory in America which makes the Tickle Me Elmo toys.
The toy laughs when you tickle it under the arm.
A new employee is hired at the Tickle Me Elmo factory and she
reports for her first day promptly at 8 am.
The next day at 08.45 there is a knock at the Personnel Manager's
door. The Foreman from the assembly line throws open the door
and begins to rant about the new employee. He complains that she
is incredibly slow and the whole line is backing up, putting the entire
production line behind schedule.

The Personnel Manager decides he should see this for himself so the
two men march down to the factory floor.
When they get there the line is so backed up that there are Tickle
Me Elmo's all over the factory floor and they're really beginning to
pile up.
At the end of the line stands the new employee surrounded by
mountains of Tickle Me Elmo's. She has a roll of plush red fabric and
a huge bag of small marbles. The 2 men watch in amazement as she
cuts a little piece of fabric, wraps it around two marbles and begins
to carefully sew the little package between Elmo's legs.
The Personnel Manager bursts into laughter. After several minutes
of hysterics he pulls himself together and approaches the woman.
"I'm sorry," he says to her, barely able to keep a straight face, "but I
think you misunderstood the instructions I gave you yesterday".
"Your job is to give Elmo two test tickles".

~~~~~~~~~~~~~~~~~~~~~~~~~~~

Settlement

"Mr. Clark, I have reviewed this case very carefully," the divorce
court Judge said, "And I've decided to give your wife $775 a week,"
"That's very fair, your honour," the husband said. "And every now
and then I'll try to send her a few bucks myself."

TALKING DOG

A guy is driving around and he sees a sign in front of a house:
"Talking Dog For Sale."
He rings the bell and the owner tells him the dog is in thebackyard.
The guy goes into the backyard and sees a Labrador retriever
sitting there.
"You talk?" he asks.
"Sure do," the Labrador replies.
"So, what's your story?"
The Lab looks up and says, "Well, I discovered that I could talk when
I was pretty young and I wanted to help the government, so I told
the CIA about my gift, and in no time at all they had me jetting from
country to country, sitting in rooms with spies and world leaders,
because no one figured a dog would be eavesdropping. I was one of
their most valuable spies for eight years running.

"But the jetting around really tired me out, and I knew I wasn't
getting any younger so I wanted to settle down. I signed up for a job
at the airport to do some undercover security work, mostly
wandering near suspicious characters and listening in.
I uncovered some incredible dealings and was awarded a batch of
medals. I got married, had a mess of puppies, and now I'm just
retired."

The guy is amazed. He goes back in and asks the owner what he
wants for the dog.
"Ten dollars." The guy says,

"This dog is amazing. Why on earth are you selling him so cheap?"
"Because he's a liar. He didn't do ANY of that shit."

Three Tortoises and a Sandwich

Mick, Andy and Roy, decide to go on a picnic.
So Mick packs the picnic basket with beer and sandwiches.
The trouble is the picnic site is ten miles away so it takes them ten days to get there.
When they get there Mick unpacks the food and beer .
'Ok Roy give me the bottle opener'
'I didn't bring it' says Roy. 'I thought you packed it'.
Mick get's worried, He turns to Andy, 'Did you bring the bottle opener?'.
Naturally Andy didn't bring it. So they're stuck ten miles from home without a bottle opener.
Mick and Andy beg Roy to go back for it. But he refuses as he says they will eat all the sandwiches. After two hours, and after they have sworn on their tortoise lives that they will not eat the sandwiches, he finally agrees.
So Roy sets off down the road at a steady pace.
20 days pass and he still isn't back and Mick and Andy are starving, but a promise is a promise.
Another 5 days and he still isn't back, but a promise is a promise.
Finally they can't take it any longer so they take out a sandwich each, and just as they are about to eat it, Roy pops up from behind a rock and shouts.

'I KNEW IT!'......I'M NOT F***ING GOING!

~~~~~~~~~~~~~~~~~~~~~~~~~~~~~

ENGLAND FC

Rumours that David Beckham was seen successfully seducing a young woman in a Spanish nightclub with a one-liner have been completely refuted by the English FA. The FA's chief publicity officer stated: "I find it totally preposterous to suggest that one of our players could make a successful pass to or at anyone."

RUNNING IN THE RAIN

A woman was having a daytime affair while her husband was at work. One wet and lusty day she was in bed with her boyfriend when, to her horror, she heard her husband's car pull into the driveway. "Oh my God - Hurry! Grab your clothes and jump out the window. My husband's home early!" "I can't jump out the window ~ It's raining out there!" "If my husband catches us in here, he'll kill us both!" she replied. "He's got a hot temper and a gun, so the rain is the least of your problems!"

So the boyfriend scoots out of bed, grabs his clothes and jumps out the window! As he ran down the street in the pouring rain, he quickly discovered he had run right into the middle of the town's annual marathon, so he started running along beside the others, about 300 of them. Being naked, with his clothes tucked under his arm, he tried to blend in as best he could. After a little while a small group of runners who had been watching him with some curiosity, jogged closer.

"Do you always run in the nude?" one asked. "Oh yes!" he replied, gasping in air. "It feels so wonderfully free!" Another runner moved alongside. "Do you always run carrying your clothes with you under your arm?" "Oh, yes" our friend answered breathlessly. "That way I can get dressed right at the end of the run and get in my car to go home! Then a third runner cast his eyes a little lower and queried. "Do you always wear a condom when you run? "Nope.........just when it's raining."

~~~~~~~~~~~~~~~~~~~~~~~~~~~

A jump-lead walks into a bar.
The barman gave it a concerned look and said "OK, I'll serve you, but don't start anything."

LITTLE FIRE TRUCK

A fire fighter is working on the engine outside the station when he notices a little girl next door in a little red wagon with little ladders hung off the sides and a garden hose tightly coiled in the middle. The girl is wearing a fire fighter's helmet. The wagon is being pulled by her dog and her cat. The fire fighter walks over to take a closer look.

"That sure is a nice fire truck," the fire fighter says with admiration. "Thanks," the girl says. The fire fighter looks a little closer and notices the girl has tied the wagon to her dog's collar and to the cat's testicles" Little Partner," the fire fighter says, "I don't want to tell you how to run your rig, but if you were to tie that rope around the cat's collar, I think you could go faster." The little girl replies thoughtfully, "You're probably right, but then I wouldn't have a siren."

~~~~~~~~~~~~~~~~~~~~~~~~~~~~

CASINO BLOND

Two bored casino dealers are waiting at the crap table.
A very attractive blonde woman arrived and bet twenty thousand Dollars on a single roll of the dice. She said, "I hope you don't mind, but I feel much luckier when I'm completely nude." With that, she stripped from the neck down, rolled the dice and yelled, "Come on, baby, Mama needs new clothes!"

As the dice came to a stop she jumped up and down and squealed..."YES! YES! I WON, I WON!"
She hugged each of the dealers and then picked up her winnings and her clothes and quickly departed.

The dealers stared at each other dumfounded.
Finally, one of them asked, "What did she roll?"
The other answered, "I don't know - I thought you were watching."

MORAL: Not all blondes are dumb, but all men are men.

Two Brothers

There were two brothers. One was very good and tried to always live right and be helpful. His brother, on the other hand, was bad and did all the things that men should not do and didn't care who he hurt.

The bad brother died. He was still missed by his brother since he loved him despite his ways. Finally, years later, the good brother died and went to Heaven. Everything was beautiful and wonderful there and he was very happy.

One day he asked God where his brother was, as he hadn't seen him there.

God said that he was sorry but his brother lived a terrible life and went to Hell instead. The good brother then asked God if there was any way for him to see his brother. So God gave him the power of vision to see into Hell and there was his brother. He was sitting on a bench with a keg of beer under one arm and a gorgeous blonde on the other.

Confused, the good brother said to God, "I am so happy that you let me into Heaven with You. It is so beautiful here and I love it. But I don't understand, if my brother was bad enough to go to Hell, why does he have the keg of beer and a gorgeous blonde. It hardly seems like a punishment".

God said unto him, "Things are not always as they seem, my son. The keg has a hole in it; the blonde does not."

~~~~~~~~~~~~~~~~~~~~~~~~~

ENGLAND FC

Q: Why aren't the England football team allowed to own a dog?
A: Because they can't hold on to a lead.

Q: What's the difference between the England team and a tea-bag?
A: The tea-bag stays in the cup longer.

The Font of St. Peter

A train hits a bus load of school girls and they all perish.
They are all in heaven trying to enter the pearly gates past St. Peter.
St. Peter asks first girl, "Karen, have you ever had any contact with a penis?"
She giggles and shyly replies, "Well I once touched the head of one with the tip of my finger."
St. Peter says, "OK, dip the tip of your finger in The Holy Water and pass through the gate."
St. Peter asks the next girl the same question, "Karina have you ever had any contact with a penis?"
The girl is a little reluctant but replies "Well once I fondled and stroked one."
St. Peter says "OK, dip your whole hand in The Holy Water and pass through the gate."
All of a sudden there is a lot of commotion in the line of girls, one girl is pushing her way to the front of the line.
When she reaches the front of the line St. Peter says "Sharon! What seems to be the rush?"
The girl replies "If I'm going to have to gargle that Holy Water, I want to do it before Tracey sticks her arse in it!!!!!!!!!!!!!!!!!!!!!!!!!"

~~~~~~~~~~~~~~~~~~~~~~~~~~~~

FANCY DRESS

A naked man with a naked girl on his back goes to a fancy dress party. The host opens the door and says,
"This is a fancy dress party, you can't come in like that!"
The man protests "I am in fancy dress, I've come as a snail."
The host says "But you've only got a naked girl on your back."
The man says "I know, it's Michelle!!"

Why Waste A Bottle of Wine?

A man enters his favourite ritzy restaurant and while sitting at his regular table, he noticed a gorgeous woman sitting at a table nearby...all alone. He calls the waiter over and asks for their most expensive bottle of wine to be sent over to her knowing that if she accepts it, she is his.

The waiter gets the bottle and quickly sends it over to the girl, saying that it is from the gentleman.

She looks at the wine and decides to send a note back to the man.

The note read: "For me to accept this bottle, you need to have a Mercedes in your garage, a million dollars in the bank, and 7 inches in your pants".

The man, after reading the note, sends one of his own notes back to her and it read:

"Just so you know - I happen to have a Ferrari Testarossa, a BMW 850il and a Mercedes CL500 in my garage; plus I have over twenty million dollars in the bank. But, not even for a woman as beautiful as you, would I cut off three inches.

Just send the bottle back."

~~~~~~~~~~~~~~~~~~~~~~~~~~

TWO COWS

Two cows were quietly chewing grass together in a field.
One cow looks up and says "MOOOO " to the other one.
"Bugger" says the other cow "I was going to say that"

The Power Of Positive Thinking

A woman who had the worst chronic headache goes to a famous "new age" holistic doctor, as a last resort. "Doctor, I have tried everything, but my headache just won't go away." The doctor replied, "You have come to the right place.
This is what I want you to do: go home, stare at yourself in the mirror, point your index fingers at your temples, and repeat this mantra: "I really don't have a headache, I really don't have a headache". Do it as long as it takes, the headache is just going to vanish."
As she leavesthe doctor's office, sceptical but curious at the same time, she tries the manoeuvre in front of the mirror in the elevator. Fingers pointed at her temples, she starts repeating "I really don't have a headache, I really don't have a headache...". She has barely said it four times, when sherealizes her headache is gone. Shocked and elated, she runs back up to the doctor. "Doctor, you are a genius! Can I please send you my husband? He's been having problems in a certain department... how can I put it..."
"When was the last time you two had sex?" the doctor asked.
"About eight years ago." she replied. "Send him over." A few days later, she is waiting with baited breath for her husband to come home from the doctor. He arrives, asks her to wait, and goes straight to the bathroom. When he comes out, he throws her on the couch and starts making wild passionate love to her, . When he's finished, he goes right back to the bathroom. A few minutes later he comes out, rouses her from her bliss and starts at it again, like an insatiable young man.
After another hour of great sex he goes and locks himself in the bathroom again. At this point the wife has become unbearably curious. She tiptoes to the bathroom door, looks through the keyhole, and sees her husband, staring at himself in the mirror, fingers pointed at his temples, repeating: "That woman is not my wife, that woman is not my wife....."

AUSSIE SLANG DICTIONARY

Abra-Kebabra:
A magic act performed on Saturday night, where fast food vanishes down the performer's throat, and then shortly afterwards, it suddenly reappears on the taxi floor.

Beer Coat:
The invisible but warm coat worn when walking home after a booze-up at 3 in the morning.

Beer Compass:
The invisible device that ensures your safe arrival home after a booze-up,even though you're too pissed to remember where you live, how you get there,and where you've come from.

Bone of Contention:
An erection that causes an argument. e.g. one that arises when a man is watching Olympic beach volleyball on TV with his girlfriend.

Millennium Domes:
The contents of a Wonderbra. i.e. extremely impressive when viewed from the outside, but there's actually f*ck-all in there worth seeing.

Mystery Bus:
The bus that arrives at the pub on Friday night while you're in the toilet after your 10th pint, and whisks away all the unattractive people so the pub is suddenly packed with stunners when you come back in.

Titanic:
A lady who goes down first time out.

Todger Dodger:
A lesbian.

Hi guys. We've all been putting in long hours recently but we've really come together as a group and I love that! However, while we are fighting a jihad, we can't forget to take care of the cave, and frankly I have a few concerns:

First of all, while it's good to be concerned about cruise missiles, we should be even more concerned about the dust in our cave. We want to avoid excessive dust inhalation, (a health and safety issue) - so we need to sweep the cave daily. I've done my bit on the cleaning rota ...have you? I've posted a sign-up sheet near the cave reception area (next to the halal toaster).

Second, it's not often I make a video address but when I do, I'm trying to scare the s**t out of most of the world's population, okay? That means that while we're taping, please do not ride your scooter in the background or keep doing the 'Wassup' thing. Thanks.

Third: Food. I bought a box of Dairylea recently, clearly wrote "Ossy" on the front, and put it on the top shelf. Today, two of my Dairylea slices were gone. Consideration. That's all I'm saying.

Fourth: I'm not against team spirit and all that, but we must distance ourselves from the Infidel's bat and ball games. Please do not chant "Ossy, Ossy, Ossy, Oy, Oy, Oy" when I ride past on the donkey. Thanks.

Five: Graffiti. Whoever wrote "OSAMA F*CKS DONKEYS" on the group toilet wall It's a lie, the donkey backed into me, whilst I was relieving myself at the edge of the mountain.

Six: The use of chickens is strictly for food. Assam, the old excuse that the 'chicken backed into me, whilst I was relieving myself at the edge of the mountain' will not be accepted in future. (With donkeys, there is a grey area.)

Finally, we've heard that there may be Western soldiers in disguise trying to infiltrate our ranks. I want to set up patrols to look for them. First patrol will be Omar, Muhammad, Abdul, Akbar and Dave.

Love you lots,
Group Hug.
Os.
PS - I'm sick of having "Osama's Bed Linen" scribbled on my laundry bag. Cut it out, it's not funny anymore

Two Prawns

Far away in the tropical waters of the Caribbean, two prawns were swimming around in the sea - one called Justin and the other called Christian. The prawns were constantly being harassed and threatened by sharks that patrolled the area. Finally one day Justin said to Christian, "I'm bored and frustrated at being a prawn, I wish I was a shark, then I wouldn't have any worries about being eaten." As Justin had his mind firmly on becoming a predator, a mysterious cod appears and says, "Your wish is granted", and lo and behold, Justin turned into a shark. Horrified, Christian immediately swam away, afraid of being eaten by his old mate. Time went on (as it invariably does...) and Justin found himself becoming bored and lonely as a shark. All his old mates simply swam away whenever he came close to them.

Justin didn't realise that his new menacing appearance was the cause of his sad plight. While out swimming alone one day he sees the mysterious cod again and can't believe his luck. Justin figured that the fish could change him back into a prawn. He begs the cod to change him back so, lo and behold, he is turned back into a prawn. With tears of joy in his tiny little eyes, Justin swam back to his friends and bought them all a cocktail. Looking around the gathering at the reef, he searched for his old pal. "Where's Christian?" he asked. "He's at home, distraught that his best friend changed sides to the enemy and became a shark", came the reply. Eager to put things right again and end the mutual pain and torture, he set off to Christian's house. As he opened the coral gate the memories came flooding back. He banged on the door and shouted, "It's me, Justin, your old friend, come out and see me again. Christian replied "No way man, you'll eat me. You're a shark, the enemy and I'll not be tricked." Justin cried back "No, I'm not. That was the old me. I've changed.".....................
"I've found Cod. I'm a prawn again Christian!!"

PREVENTS DISEASE....

Miss Bea, the church organist, was in her eighties and had never been married. She was much admired for her sweetness and kindness to all.
The pastor came to call on her one afternoon early in the spring, and she welcomed him into her Victorian parlor. She invited him to have a seat while she prepared a little tea.

As he sat facing her old pump organ, the young minister noticed a cut glass bowl sitting on top of it, filled with water. In the water floated, of all things, a condom. Imagine his shock and surprise. Imagine his curiosity! Surely Miss Bea had flipped or something!

When she returned with tea and cookies, they began to chat. The pastor tried to stifle his curiosity about the bowl of water and its strange floater, but soon it got the better of him, and he could resist no longer.

"Miss Bea," he said, "I wonder if you would tell me about this?" (pointing to the bowl).

"Oh, yes," she replied, "isn't it wonderful? I was walking downtown last fall and I found this little package on the ground. The directions said to put it on the organ, keep it wet, and it would prevent disease. And you know, I haven't had a cold all winter."

A Boost for the Welsh Film Industry!

Now that Catherine Zeta-Jones-Douglas has become firmly established in Hollywood, the Welsh film industry is to receive additional funding to step up production. They are going to remake many well known films, but this time with a Welsh flavour. The following are planned for release next year...

* 9 ½ Leeks

* Trefforest Gump

* An American Werewolf in Powys

* Huw Dares Gwyneth

* Dai Hard

* The Wizard of Oswestry

* The Eagle has Llandudno

* The Magnificent Severn

* Haverfordwest Was Won

* Austin Powys

* The Magic Rhonddabout

* Independence Dai

* The Bridge on the River Wye

* A Beautiful Mind-you

* **The Welsh Patient**

* **The King and Dai**

* **The Sheepshag Redemption**

* **Breakfast at Taffynys**

* **Look You Back in Bangor**

* **Evans Can Wait**

* **A Fishguard Called Rhondda**

* **Where Eagles Aberdare**

* **Dial M For Merthyr**

* **Sheepless in Seattle**

* **Lawrence of Llandybie**

* **Seven Brides from Seven Sisters**

* **Welsh Connection**

* **Welsh Connection II**

* **The Lost Boyos**

and finally..........

* **The Llanfairpwllgwyngyllgogerychwyrndrobwllllantysiliogogogoch That Time Forgot**

Now there's lovely !!!

Why men are just happier people

Your last name stays put.
The garage is all yours.
Wedding plans take care of themselves.
Chocolate is just another snack.
You can never be pregnant.
You can wear a white T-shirt to a water park.
You can wear NO T-shirt to a water park.
Car mechanics tell you the truth.
The world is your urinal.
You don't have to think of which way to turn a nut on a bolt.
Same work, more pay.
Wrinkles add character.
Wedding dress - £2,000. Morning suit rental - £150.
People never stare at your chest when you're talking to them.
The occasional well-rendered belch is practically expected.
New shoes don't cut, blister or mangle your feet.
One mood - all the time.
Phone conversations are over in 30 seconds flat.
A five-day vacation requires only one suitcase.
You can open all your own jars.
You get extra credit for the slightest act of thoughtfulness.
If someone forgets to invite you, he or she can still be your friend.
Your underwear is £8.95 for a three-pack.
Three pairs of shoes are more than enough.
You never have strap problems in public.
You are unable to see wrinkles in your clothes.
Everything on your face stays its original colour.
The same hairstyle lasts for years, maybe decades.
You only have to shave your face and neck.
You can play with toys all your life.
Your belly usually hides your big hips.
One wallet, one pair of shoes, one colour for all seasons.
You can wear shorts no matter how your legs look.
You can "do" your nails with a pen-knife.
You have freedom of choice concerning growing a moustache.
You can do Christmas shopping for 25 relatives on December 24th in 25 minutes.

And finally, remember...

As a Wise Man once said to me...

"Its better to be pissed off than pissed on!"

Can you do better?

A collection of stories like these takes a long time to put together and there will always be people that know lots of better jokes and stories than these and will never be able to publish them.

Well, now you can!!

The PPGS publishing team is already well into the next collection and if you would like to submit a joke for book 4, and we publish it, we will give you a credit and send you a free copy of the next book.

Please send your joke or story, in writing to:

PPGS, PO Box 42, Princes Risborough, Bucks.HP27 0XH

If you would like to be informed when the next book is due out and perhaps have a copy reserved, please write to the address above or email to info@kcs-solutions.co.uk

We still have a few copies of Book 2 available (The Most Hilarious After Dinner Jokes & Stories)– if you have missed it and would like one sent to you, just write or email us and we will send you a copy whilst stocks last.

(Sorry; our first book - The Most Outrageous After Dinner Jokes & Stories has now completely sold out)